Laurie didn't exactly get a warm welcome when she arrived on the tropical island of Mondego. The only person who seemed to be prepared to be kind was the lordly Marquez de Velho Barreiro – and his kindness was of a lordly, lofty sort that seemed to mark all too clearly the distance between them.

THE WHITE OLEANDER

BY

KATHRYN BLAIR

MILLS & BOON LIMITED
17–19 FOLEY STREET
LONDON W1A 1DR

All the characters in this book have no existence outside the imagination of the Author, and have no relation whatsoever to anyone bearing the same name or names. They are not even distantly inspired by any individual known or unknown to the Author, and all the incidents are pure invention.

This edition 1974

ISBN 0 263 71641 4

Made and printed in Great Britain by
C. Nicholls & Company Ltd
The Philips Park Press, Manchester

CHAPTER ONE

THE LONG beige car purred up from the quay on to the esplanade, passed a string of shops with wide cement porticoes and swung between square-cut pillars to curve round the drive and arrive at the white and gold entrance of the Hotel Carnac. The swarthy chauffeur in the slate blue uniform slid from his seat and opened the back door. Laurie Fielding stepped out, stared at the intricate tiling of the porch and at the spotless white suits of two very black African porters, and quelled an impulse to rub her eyes.

So she was at last on the island of Mondego, and this was actually the hotel whose name had looked so romantic on the envelope when she had written to Stella. Senhora Eduardo Alvares, Hotel Carnac, Porto, Ilha Mondego. An exciting name and address for one's own sister; even more exciting now that one realized the splendor of the place in which she lived.

As Laurie entered the dim, cool vestibule her heart was beating high. It was five years since she had seen Stella, and the letters from Portugal and Brazil, from Mozambique and Angola, had been infrequent and uninformative. Even her last letter had conveyed very little beside the fact that Laurie would be met at the boat and addressed as "Miss Bell." "That's very important, Laurie," Stella had reiterated; "I'll explain when I see you."

Well it wouldn't be long now before she would know the wonderful satisfaction of being greeted by the sister she had loved so much in childhood, and learn all about this "Miss Bell" mystery.

She and Stella had never been really close, of course, because the years betwen them had constituted too great a gap for Laurie to leap, and Stella's patience had not been of the sisterly kind. But they were both grown up now, which surely would level out the differences between them, both in age and nature. Laurie knew in her bones that it was going to be grand to live with Stella and do a thoroughly good job of work at the same time. It was like a miracle to have this happen at a phase in her existence when she was longing for just a speck of spice to liven her days. The sea voyage alone had provided enough small excitements to last quite a while, and now she was to live among the people of Mondego . . .

At this point in her thoughts Laurie became awere that a resplendent Portuguese, probably the hotel manager himself, was smiling and bowing at her elbow.

"Ah, yes senhora, you are Miss Bell. The Senhora Alvares is expecting you. Will you please come to the lift?"

Instructions were given to the thin black lift boy. The lift hummed the brief distance to the upper floor, and Laurie was escorted from it to a tall door at the end of a corridor, which was opened by a small, dark-haired maid. She spoke in perfect English.

"You will please enter, Miss Bell. I will tell the senhora you are here."

To Laurie, everything about her still had the intangible quality of a brilliant dream. The lounge in which she found herself was huge and two massive french doors were wide open to a long balcony which looked over the courtyard and a line of ornamental palms to the sea; a sea vividly blue with a frill of white where it met the bleached sand and lazily licked around an assortment of native boats.

She stared curiously about her. The furnishings were of the costly and comfortable kind natural to luxury hotels, the curtaining a heavy cream silk damask thickly lined with white, against the sun. But the flowers banked high at one end of the room were purely Stella. She had always been clever with flowers, Laurie remembered; a moorland posy had acquired significance and sophistication whenever Stella had bothered to arrange one in the little house on the edge of York. These flowers were large and exotic, shading from pale pink-tan gladiolus, through great orange-colored masses of unindentifiable blossoms to the dark and ruddy sprays of flame-flower.

On a table between the two french windows branches of wax-white oleanders stood out from a bronze bowl against a pink-tinted mirror. The effect was startling and beautiful;

in fact, Laurie's grey eyes still shone with the wonder of it when she turned round at the sound of an opening door.

It was an unforgettable moment. Stella stood framed in the doorway, a slim and lovely figure in a turquoise hostess gown buttoned from throat to hem with big, scintillating pearls. The ashen hair, brushed back and pinned into silky curls, framed a face of absolute fairness and almost aquiline beauty. She was like, yet unlike, the sister Laurie had known. For fully a minute Laurie experienced the aching admiration of her girlhood.

"Hello, Stella," she said a little awkwardly, and involuntarily it was she who moved forward.

Stella received her kiss, pressed her arm and indicated the room behind her. "Come into my bedroom. We shan't be interrupted there."

"My luggage is at the customs office."

"We'll deal with it later."

Stella could deal with anything, Laurie felt. She had always been like that, right through childhood; even when she had started to train as a nurse and loathed it, Stella had found a marvellous way of leaving the hospital and turning her knowledge to account.

Laurie followed her sister into a bedroom of enormous dimensions. Twin beds with quilted, rose-pink covers, soft white mosquito nets drawn back and tied with rose-pink bows; a wall-fan gently whirring, flowers quivering, gleaming surfaces of walnut, a wide dressing table covered with crystal jars and bowls, and a deep rich carpet of rose and cream.

Stella waved to a large chair and herself sank in to a stool in front of the array of expensive cosmetics. "The snapshot you sent didn't do you justice, Laurie. You're quite pretty." Her voice was lower, her diction even more perfect than Laurie recalled. "You look awfully young, though, I don't believe I looked so young at twenty."

"It's a nuisance looking young. Father says. . . ."

"Oh, yes." The note of reserve in Stella's manner became more noticeable. "How is he?"

Laurie's eyes softened. "He's happy. Your sending him money every quarter has made so much difference, because now he can afford to put an occasional real antique in the shop window. He bought some old Venetian goblets last month and they sold almost at once for a good figure. He sent you his love, of course, and a kiss for his grandson. I'm longing to see Richard, myself."

Stella did not answer this. She raised slender, white, pink-tipped fingers and gently stroked her jaw, watching her reflection as she did so. Vanity and grace were in her every line. Laurie pondered. Stella was only twenty-eight and she now had everything she had ever wanted: a rich husband, a small son, and a dazzling loveliness. Yet there was something which apparently eluded her, some tiny fly in the amber of her content.

"I expect you think I"m horribly cold and offhand," said Stella, "particularly as we haven't seen each other for so long. Don't conclude that I'm not glad to see you. I am—very glad indeed." A pause. "I suppose you thought it odd my not meeting you?"

"I was a little disappointed, but the elegant chauffeur made your apologies. Is he really yours—*and* that long car which seems to float on a cloud?"

Her eagerness brought a smile to Stella's carefully reddened lips. "Yes, they're mine; and when I go away I shall leave them here, for you and Richard to use." For the first time her expression lost its hardness. "He's an adorable child, Laurie—nearly three and exceptionally good-looking. You'll take every care of him, won't you?"

"He's my only nephew. I'm going to love him."

Stella drew in her lip. As she twisted back to the mirror the smile faded. "Your training at the Hollinshead Home did include sick nursing as well as ordinary care, didn't it?"

"I had several months in the ward, and for the rest of the time I shared charge of the toddlers; it was pretty comprehensive. I wrote you that my training was complete and I was due for promotion."

"You don't know what a relief it was to hear that you were fully trained and willing to travel out here. I've been so terribly worried about Richard, and I don't know where to look for a really good nurse. I've tried the Portuguese, but they don't go in for such sound, systematic training as we do, and there's the language difficulty. He's been travelling round with Eduardo and me, and a retinue of servants, living at hotels or at the houses of our friends. He's not at all strong and it's been bad for him."

"Poor sweet," said Laurie softly. "With me he'll lead an uneventful existence, the kind that a child really enjoys best. It's a pity you haven't a cottage here, so that I could take over preparing his food as well."

"We're looking into that. Mondego is hot but it's peaceful. I feel I could leave him here with you. I trust you, Laurie."

She got up. The brocade of her gown whispered as she went over to pull shut the door to the balcony. She turned and was outlined against the mild-morning sunshine, her face shadowed and the china blue eyes unreadable.

"Aren't you curious as to why I insisted that you be called "Miss Bell'?"

"I was, but I'd forgotten it in the excitement of meeting you. I like Fielding better."

"I'm afraid," said Stella deliberately, "that you will never be anything but 'Miss Bell' in Mondego."

A chill feathered across Laurie's skin; the first chill of premonition and disillusionment. Her sister's tone had the metallic brusqueness of a wealthy woman dealing with an inferior. Fleetingly Laurie tried to excuse the manner. Stella was accustomed to mixing with the upper social strata, and to being surrounded by obsequious servants; it had temporarily slipped her mind that Laurie was not an underling.

"It sounds mysterious," she managed brightly.

Stella spoke with the same curt inflection. "I'm going to be honest with you, Laurie. You won't like what I have to tell you, but I'll go back to the beginning, to try and make you understand. Do you recall the circumstances of my leaving England?"

"Why, yes. Mrs. Bentinck-Jones was incurably ill and you got the job of accompanying her to the south of France as her nurse-companion."

"That's so. We went to Cannes, and life there, after the various sorts of restrictions in England, was so amazingly good that I took a lot of trouble over Mrs. Bentinck Jones, with the result that when she died a few months later I came into five hundred pounds."

"Good Lord. That was something like a reward!"

"I earned it," said Stella crisply. "It was *my* money and I saw no reason to share it with you and Father."

"I'm sure neither of us would have taken a penny!" Laurie put in swiftly, with spirit. "Daddy accepts money from you now because you have plenty, but I don't expect any bigger salary from you that I'd get in England. I didn't come here as a poor relative to cling to the fringe of your prosperity. For heaven's sake don't get that idea."

Stella shrugged. "I was talking of the past when, to me, five hundred pounds was riches. I didn't have to wonder what to do with it because Mrs. Bentinck-Jones was a generous and considerate woman; she had instructed a local lawyer that I was to remain at the hotel at her expense for three months after her death. She thought I'd deserved such a holiday after the trying time I had with her."

Laurie said, "She must have been a dear person. I wish you'd told us about it, though so that we could have been thrilled for you."

Stella frowned. She came to sit on the arm of a chair, and smoothed the silk cuff of her gown with slow, calculating fingers. "Neither you nor Father are my kind, Laurie. You're both simple and not very ambitious, and everything I did was for my own betterment—even to the way I nursed the old lady. The hotel in Cannes was like this one, but bigger and full of monied holiday-makers from all over the Continent, and I determined that during those three months I'd not only have a high time but find a wealthy husband. That strikes you as cold-blodded, doesn't it?"

"It *was* cold-blooded."

"To you, yes. You're the type to fall in love with someone penniless and happily share a garret; but I couldn't go back to living the hard way. I wanted all those things that girls like us can only acquire by marriage. I wanted money and position, and I went all out to get them—bought nice clothes and was seen everywhere. I gambled a little at the Casino and discreetly made enquiries about people staying at other hotels. There were many playboys but no potential husbands, till Eduardo Alvares came and took a suite at my hotel. It was the greatest luck in the world." There was a queer, reminiscent flash in her eyes as if she were recollecting a tough and subtle battle, well won. "You don't yet know these Portuguese — how difficult and conventional they are, their ingrained prejudice against too much freedom for women. Eduardo was nearly forty and instinctively, once I'd contrived an introduction to him, I knew there could be only one way of handling him. He was attracted by my fairness and terribly concerned about my being alone. I made the utmost use of both."

Laurie hardly dared to breathe. Almost, she sensed the unpleasantness to come. "Was he in love with you?"

Stella nodded. "But I took no chances. He's of the aristocracy — his closest friend is the Marquez de Velho Barreiro — and I daren't risk telling him that my father owned a shop in a York by-street."

Laurie was fairly intuitive. She could see the Stella of four or five years ago; pathetically young, alone and lovely, hesitantly confiding to the rich Portuguese the myth that she was the last of an old but impoverished English family. From some it might ring false, but not from Stella. She would mention it lightly, with a grief-tinged smile, and hurriedly pass on to something else. The wistful English girl untrained to be anything but the wife of a rich man, but bravely bearing up. A superb piece of acting. Laurie was astonished at the bitterness which rose in a lump in her throat.

"So you told him that you had no father—no relations at all," she said in a voice gone cold with hurt. "Your Eduardo isn't aware of my existence."

"I'm merely informing you, not asking you to set yourself up as a judge," Stella answered sharply. "I've no regrets — not one. I'm happy with Eduardo, and we live in a way that suits me very well. I like getting around the world and meeting people, I like fabulous jewels and clothes, and I haven't been a cheat. He has a wife and a son and considers himself entirely blessed." When Laurie made as if to speak, Stella stood up and gestured decisively.

"I've thought up all the romantic, threadbare arguments and they don't interest me. Whether he would have married me whatever my background, I'll never know — and I never want to know. At the time I risked everything to get him."

"But can't you be honest with him now?"

Stella's whole being tightened and her voice went almost harsh. "You haven't the faintest idea what you're suggesting. Knowledge of that kind would come between us like a frightful grey ghost. All our friends, both English and Portuguese, are in the very highest circles; Eduardo has estates in Portugal and others in the Portuguese colonies. One of his largest is only a hundred miles away, in Portuguese East Africa. You must see how it is, Laurie!"

Yes, Laurie saw. It had been wrong of Stella to base her marriage on falsehood, but Eduardo's happiness had to be considered now, and the little boy's. It was cool of Stella to invite her young sister to be Richard's nurse; cool but utterly typical, and to some extent comprehensible. The woman who had hooked Eduardo Alvares could have anticipated no difficulty with Laurie Fielding. Yet Laurie's heart revolted, more for the slight to her father than for herself. Henry Fielding might not be a success by wordly standards, but he was kind and candid, and he loved the beautiful and the rare; above all, he loved his daughters.

"I think I do understand," Laurie said slowly. "What, exactly, are you asking of me?"

"Your silence about our relationship — you have a father, but I haven't. For the rest I'm not asking, I'm *giving*. You'll live luxuriously in a part of the world you could never otherwise have hoped to visit. You'll be Miss Bell — I chose the name because it's easy to remember by the staff — and your only duties will be looking after Richard. Apart from him you won't be restricted in any way."

"Aren't you afraid," enquired Laurie curiously, "that I'll let you down? You know I'm against deception, yet you're willing to leave Richard here on the island with me while you go away with your husband. Don't you think you're taking rather a long chance?"

Stella drew a sigh as if the worst were over. She took a cigarette from a carved white jade box on a bedside table and flicked a gold lighter. Through a lazy veil of smoke she said evenly. "You won't let me down, Laurie. As a child you were fanatically loyal, and you haven't changed. No one else will suspect that Richard is your nephew, but you'll treasure the fact — you're made that way. That's why I wanted you to come—because an affectionate aunt who is also a trained child's nurse is a double insurance for his welfare."

"I see. But aren't you a little frightened that someone may spot a likeness between you and me?"

"I've considered that. We're not very alike; you favor father physically as well as mentally. Your coloring is brown-gold, your eyes are grey and you're at least two inches shorter than I. The difference in our dress and demeanour will do the rest. But to provide against . . . accidents, I'm compelled to make a stipulation. Only you and I know that we're sisters, so that if any rumor should circulate it will be obvious where it started. I shall deny it, naturally, and my word will carry more weight than yours. As well as denying all connection with you and sending you away, I shall stop the allowance I've been posting to father."

She had spoken so moderately that it took Laurie a minute or two to appreciate her meaning. Then a flush dyed her cheeks, and it seemed as if the last shred of all joy and expectation which had mounted during the journey down the East Coast of Africa went out like a blown candle flame. She got quickly to her feet.

"That's . . . hateful," she said, above the pounding of her heart. "You're ruthless, Stella, and unprincipled."

"On the contrary, Im merely anxious to protect my marriage and my child. Don't be silly about this, Laurie. My proposition is wholly to your advantage. I've been frank with you, and you can't blame me if I keep an ace up my sleeve. I shouldn't have a second's peace if I didn't." Negligently, she tapped ash into a crystal tray. "Before we go any further you'd better meet Richard."

"I can't—not yet." She had to get out of this perfumed and sultry atmosphere, go somewhere where it was possible to think. "Have I a room in this hotel?"

"Where else? It's the only one on Mondego." Stella extracted a key from a bedside table drawer and swung it by the metal disc. "I'm sorry to have had to greet you with all this, but it had to be rushed through before you encountered anyone else. Eduardo is out, but he'll be back at noon because we have a party coming for lunch. You'll meet him then. Go to your room, by all means — it's Number Seventeen, opposite the lift. I'll ring below and tell them to send you a cup of chocolate, and when you've had a rest we'll talk again. You must tell me what sort of trip you had, and how it feels to land straight from England on an African island."

Her level tones seemed to echo out into the corridor as Laurie quickly crossed the lounge and went out. She walked blindly, stumbled in the thick-piled carpet, and automatically turned left, down the wide staircase. She needed air and space in which to breathe; more than anything she needed time.

Without looking to right or left in the vestibule, she hastened out into the sunshine. Heat smote her in a wave, but she was hardly conscious of it. Hurried walking took her away from the esplanade and up over a coastal road shaded by palms and nut trees. She dragged off her hat and pushing shaking fingers through her sweat-damp hair.

This was really horrible, and it had happened so suddenly that she still quivered from the shock. Stella should have prepared her — put something into her letter which would, at last, have shown her that this was no case of an elder sister being sweet to a young one. But Stella never took the smallest risk of failure. For her son she wanted a nurse she could implicitly trust, one who would go to any lengths for his well-being, and who better qualified for such a post than sister Laurie? Lovely, selfish Stella, whose only grace was a deep, unshakable love for Richard.

Laurie slowed. Yes, judging by the way she spoke of him Stella did love the child, and for that one could forgive her a great deal. Poor little rich boy, surrounded by Portuguese servants, bedded in costly toys yet without a playmate or even anyone who might guess that he was beginning to notice things beyond his own world and to form his own baby conclusions.

Laurie unbuttoned her cream linen jacket, pressed a handkerchief to her streaming temples and blinked her aching eyes. But she did not muse upon the wisdom of walking during the hottest part of the day on the sub-tropical, Portuguese island of Mondego.

She was thinking of her father on the quay at Southampton, his smiling, "I'm a dilatory correspondent, Laurie, but I shall look for your letters regularly and I know you won't let me down."

Stella might not write to him for months together and then pen only a few words to accompany a cheque on an English bank, but he had always been proud of her beauty and believed the very best of her. That he should learn the truth and that the allowance she made him should cease was unthinkable.

Had she an alternative to Stella's plan? What if she undertook to maintain secrecy but refused to stay in the island—would Stella have the decency to acknowledge herself defeated? Perhaps, but she would not resist the acid pleasure of withholding the cheque for Henry Fielding, and her father had come so much to depend on it. She would stab at Laurie in the place where it was most likely to hurt.

Mechanically, Laurie went on walking down the dusty road which now stretched ahead like a pale scar in the lush green growth of the coastal belt. Between the thickets there were ultramarine glimpses of the Indian Ocean, and almost detachedly Laurie saw the thatched conical roofs of native huts whose mud walls were screened from the road by thickly-sown agaves which had sent up their trees of flowers. At one point piccanins peeped from behind bushes, but otherwise the road was singularly deserted.

The sun and humidity were beginning to sap her energy, but she went on moving in an unhappy langour, carrying with her the inescapable problem. Impossible to come to a decision yet; the situation was too painfully new.

She had been walking for three-quarters of an hour when a cloud of sand-colored dust appeared ahead. The car causing it was a big, luxurious affair in amethyst and chromium, even more spectacular than Stella's turn-out, and it approached so swiftly that she had hardly decided to get well off the road to avoid the dust when it braked, not three yards away.

The driver got out. He wore immaculate white drill and the white silk collar of his shirt lay open to reveal a mahogany brown throat. He was big; tall, but not exceptionally so, and when he bowed she saw that his hair was almost black, springing in a short wave from a point at the centre of his forehead; thick, attractive hair.

He said something rapidly in Portuguese, and she shook her head.

"I beg your pardon, senhor, but I don't know your language."

"Oh. You are English," he said, with an alien emphasis on the consonants. "Perhaps you do not realize that there is no town in this road before Villa Barreiro, which is four kilos away."

She met eyes that were very dark with lights in them; aloof eyes which regarded her disinterestedly. Inexplicably, she hardened.

"I am walking for pleasure, senhor."

His manner changed, subtly, but was hardly warmer. "You are a tourist?"

"A visitor," she corrected him.

"Staying in Porto Mondego? You surely have not walked from the town in this temperature!"

Laurie swallowel. She was overheated and sticky, the cream linen suit clung where it touched, and she was hazy with unhappiness besides. The keen glance must have taken in her pallor, for he said, almost peremptorily:

"I will take you back to Porto Mondego."

"Thank you, senhor, but I prefer to walk."

Apparently no woman, or man for that matter, had ever before refused his assistance. He seemed to tighten up, and a sudden cold, mocking brilliance showed in those dark eyes.

"I do not know you, senhora," he said calmly, "and you do not know me, but you happen to be in Mondego, where young ladies do not roam the roads like *gitanos*. You do not wish to ride back to the town with me, and I confess it may make me late for an appointment to take you; nevertheless, you will please get into the car!"

Temporarily witless, she gazed up at features so distinctively handsome as to be nearly incredible. His cheekbones were high, his nose not quite so regular in line as the rest of his features, and the well-cut mouth and angular chin had all the fearlessness attributed to those medieval courtiers who made Portugal illustrious and romantic. Perhaps it was his tan which accentuated the extraordinary whiteness of his teeth.

She had heard about violent Portuguese and amorous Portuguese but never of the chilly, commanding type. There and then she decided she didn't care for it.

Even more politely than before she said, "I am accustomed to walking, senhor, and I enjoy it very much. I needn't detain you."

"So?" It was a dismissive syllable, as if what she had said were of no consequence. His shoulders rose in a shrug. "You are newly arrived in Mondego?"

"I arrived this morning on the inter-island mail boat from Mauritis."

A comprehending lift of the brow. "And how long do you stay?"

"I don't know. A few months — maybe longer."

"Then I suggest that it will do you no harm to acquire some of our ways." He opened the door of the back of the car. "In England you have never had to tolerate a sun as hot as this. Please get in."

Determination seemed useless against this man, but Laurie, having already borne enough frustration for one morning, felt bound to go on trying. "I *like* walking, senhor. It's kind of you, but. . . ."

He snapped his fingers as though nearing the end of his patience. "It is not kind; it is merely my duty. Do not expect me to believe that it would please you to trudge many miles in the dust and eventually reach the town too exhausted to eat lunch. To me, you do not appear robust."

Such was the nature of the man that Laurie, in her depleted condition, at last gave up and obeyed. She climbed into the car, the door clicked shut, he slipped into his place and they shot smoothly up and over the hill.

Laurie sat in the middle of the soft wide seat, encompassed in a deep and luscious richness. She hated it, because it reminded her of Stella. This man reminded her of Stella, too. He was of the kind her sister had mentioned, the wealthy aristocrats who thought that women should be sheltered and chaperoned wherever they went. Being Portuguese, and not having been properly introduced, he could not, of course, have her beside him; that would have been altogether too unconventional.

But now that he had his own way he was cooly charming. "If you are here for a few months you will have time to become closely acquainted with the island," he was saying in pleasant, foreign tones. "There is much to see and learn and also a great deal which you will find entertaining. You have, perhaps, a distant relative in Mondego?"

"A friend," she answered conservatively.

"I thought it must be so. It is obvious that you have no drop of Portuguese blood."

"Would you call that a drawback, senhor?"

A faint amusement came into his voice. "It would anger you if I did. You have the fierce independence of the British, and I will not rouse it again, particularly as we are now entering Porto Mondego. I know most of these people. With whom are you staying?"

Laurie could not tell him. The idea of explaining herself to this man as Miss Bell, nurse to Richard Alvares, was so repugnant that she shivered inside the hot dampness of her clothes. She had only to get away from him this once; the chances were that she would never see him again.

"Will you please stop for me in the centre of the town?"

"You mean the centre of the Esplanda?"

"Please."

They swept past the hotel and within two minutes, near he statue of Dom Henrique, he braked. He was out on the white road, opening her door, distant and unsmiling once more. For a second she felt his touch at her elbow as he helped her out. Then he bowed stiffly, and somehow the Portuguese in him became much more marked.

"When next you wish for a stroll take with you a companion and a thick sunshade, and do not choose a road such as that one. In Mondego we have splendid gardens where the ladies walk. And please remember that there are few in this island who comprehend the English disregard of the proprieties. *Adeus, senhora!*"

He got back into the car, it swerved round in a circle and sped away up the esplanade.

CHAPTER TWO

Laurie paused on the pavement. The shops were closing for lunch and siesta, and she supposed she ought to return to the hotel, face Stella again and admit she had no option but to fall in with her wishes. After all, once she was used to knowing where she stood, her situation would matter much less. She had actually come out from England to be a nurse to Richard, and neither Stella nor anyone else would be able to detract from her enjoyment of the exotic island. Richard needed her. She would have the child and the prodigal extravagance of Mondego; a job to do in a breathtaking environment. A good many girls would have given anything for such an opportunity.

Oddly, as she made her way between lazing Africans and smart young Portuguese, it was of the man in the car that she thought. She hadn't liked his impersonality or his invulnerable dignity. Also, there had been something in his manner which was not quite so Portuguese as his looks; of that she was certain, though she had no intention of dissecting the certainty.

She entered the hotel, ignored the lift and went up the staircase. She took the key from her pocket and unlocked the door of Number Seventeen. Inside the room she stood still. Her trunk and suitcase were there, her name on the labels obliterated by black crayon. A massive bouquet of mixed flowers stood in a large jar on the fruitwood dressing table, and beside it rested the portrait of a grave-eyed, curly-haired little boy.

Laurie did not pick up the portrait as Stella had doubtless intended. She turned from it, placed her hat and jacket on the willow-green bed-cover and washed at the basin. She brushed her hair, dusted her face with powder and used a rub of lipstick. Her frocks needed ironing before she could change, so she slipped back again into the jacket, gave it a pat here and there and dispassionately viewed her image in the mirror.

She felt so much older than the girl who had stepped from the coastal boat this morning that her reflection was vaguely surprising and heartening. It was simply a serious young face framed by soft brownish curls; perhaps the grey eyes were shadowed, but that would pass off as she became inured to her new status. She wasn't so very different from Laurie Fielding of York.

She had just taken a clean handkerchief from her bag when Stella came in. Stella ravishing and regal in pure white silk, with a string of aquamarines at her throat and a shorter one interspersed with diamonds at her wrist. She spoke in those level, unhurried tones with which Laurie was becoming familiar.

"So you went out, Laurie? That's rather unwise here at midday. but you were a little upset perhaps and in a way the walk did you good. We always used to say that a tramp over the moors stabilized one's perspective." A brief silence. Then, pointedly, "Is everything all right now?"

Composedly, Laurie answered, "Yes, everything's all right. It was a blow, but I'll live it down."

"Good." A shade of relief lighted Stella's tones. "You won't be sorry, I promise you. You'll make friends here. There are quite a number of young people who will accept you simply because you're English, even though your position is of the paid type. The young ones aren't high-hat, and you don't have to lie about anything."

"Only live a lie," said Laurie.

"You won't be harming anyone by it — the reverse, in fact." She hesitated. "There's one thing more. I can't have you form an attachment for anyone here. Friendship, if you like, but nothing serious. It's possible that one of these young men will fall for you because you're different from the local women, but you mustn't let anything develop, or other complications will arise, and I won't have that. Life here can be smooth and untroubled, if you'll let it."

"Don't worry," Laurie told her a trifle wearily. "From what I've seen of Portuguese men since landing at nine-thirty this morning, I can assure you that I wouldn't marry one of them if he were the last man on earth."

Stella smiled. "That's the correct attitude, but I doubt if you'll keep it up. The Portuguese *fidalgo* can be fascinating — but he's also hidebound where marriage is concerned. He seldom marries out of his class. Well . . . are you ready to meet my husband and Richard?"

Laurie's decision was made, and the very thought that she need no longer struggle against the loss of her illusions dispersed some of the heaviness which had gathered about her heart. She had expected too much from Stella, that was it. Marriage and riches don't necessarily change a woman's character; in Stella's case they had merely strengthened her ego and diminished the importance of those outside her circle. And Laurie was now and for ever one of those on the outside.

She followed Stella into the lounge, saw a man in informal but impeccable pearl-grey flannels pouring drinks at a table. Stella gave a purring laugh, said a few words in Portuguese, then laid her fingertips on Laurie's forearm.

"Eduardo, this is Miss Bell. I told you she would be here this morning. She looks everything we desire in a nurse for Richard, doesn't she?"

He bowed slightly; a dark-skinned, thickset man of just above middle height. His smile was kind and interested; it showed good teeth, one of which was gold-topped. "You are very welcome here, Miss Bell. I trust you had a good voyage?"

He was nice! "Excellent, thank you, senhor," Laurie answered gratefully.

"I have arranged for Miss Bell to have lunch up here with Richard," said Stella. "Anita is changing his clothes in his bedroom, so he should be ready soon. Perhaps you had better go down to our friends, darling, and I will follow as soon as I have made the little introduction."

"Felipe is here, my dear. He left the others below in the lounge."

"Did I hear my name, Eduardo?" A tall figure appeared from the balcony. "Ah, Stella!" He took her hand, cast a quick, appreciative glance at her exquisite appearance and bent to place his lips to her wrist. "Always you grow more beautiful. I tell Eduardo he is the most fortunate man on earth."

"Because he married an Englishwoman?" Stella used the continental coin of coquetry; the sidelong glance, a featherweight caress in her voice. "Your own father did that, Felipe."

He was looking at Laurie, politely and utterly without recognition. According to his code, apparently, they had never really met. It was Eduardo, not Stella, who cordially set matters right.

"At last we have someone who will know exactly how to care for our Richard," he said. "Miss Bell arrived here from England this morning." He turned to her. "May I present the Marquez de Velho Barreiro."

Laurie had to stiffen her lips to still a tremor of astonishment and vexation; then she forced them into a smile.

The Marquez bowed. "I am happy to know you, Miss Bell. Possibly you are finding Mondego a great change from England?"

For a moment she wondered if the wording he had chosen were intended to remind her of their brief exchange half an hour ago. But she rejected the notion; he was altogether too exalted to care. Yet his look was faintly sardonic.

She murmured something which Stella cut short.

"Perhaps you will go and find Richard yourself, Miss Bell? I am sure you will have no difficulty in making yourself known to him. His room is through the second door." And to the men: "I think she will be very capable. Drink up, my slow ones, and let us go."

Almost the last words Laurie heard as she passed from the room were in those same clear velvety tones: "You appear pleased with yourself today, Felipe. Is one permitted to ask the reason? Did the fish bite well out there on the rocks, or have you had chocolate this morning *tete-a-tete* with a charming woman?"

"Neither, my dear Stella," came the light reply. "It is enough that I am about to enjoy an hour with you!"

Laurie, unversed in the ways of such a man, was yet percipient enough to realize that his ease in so complimenting another man's wife could only spring from a worldliness so complete that no ordinary woman could ever hope to follow him in it.

She closed the door behind her and found herself facing an open doorway through which came the subdued, staccato tones of a child. Laurie let out her pent-up feelings in a long, bewildered sigh, and summoned a cheerful smile for the meeting with her nephew.

Richard was not a merry child. He had a head of dark-brown curls and brown eyes that were bruised-looking underneath. His movements were languid and his voice had a high, drawling note which just missed being a whine. Though he was dark, in features he favored Stella rather than his father. He had her fine straight nose and pointed chin, and the pronounced cheekbones which later would contribute to adult good looks. His skin was pale and faintly sallow, but beautifully clear.

"More beef and more sleep," was Laurie's first mental comment, upon making the acquaintance of Richard Alvares. To which she afterwards added a rider to the effect that the sooner he was deprived of the pampering Portuguese servants the better. Almost every move the child made was forbidden by the maid, Anita.

"Not to climb, *pequeno*. It makes the little man tired." Or, "To play with stones is not good—the blouse get dirty. We will find your rabbit."

Anita had to be gently persuaded to mind her own business—that of being lady's maid to Stella. Other servants needed to be convinced that only one person was necessary to Richard's health and training, Laurie took the child so entirely to her heart that she hardly cared whom she snubbed in order to disperse the treacly atmosphere in which he was steeped. When a salad, ordered for his lunch, arrived blanketed in oily dressing, she sent it away and demanded separate dishes of ingredients so that she herself could mix his requirements, and she actually instructed one of the hotel chefs in the art of plain fish-steaming. He was scandalized by the British lack of imagination in cooking, but because the Alvares were such important guests he did omit the wine and cream, if not the seasoning.

Laurie did not hope for quick results from the changes in Richard's diet and upbringing. Children, she knew well, are very much creatures of habit and her chief concern, to begin with, was gradually to break down the bad habits and replace them with good ones; all would come right in time. He was young enough, thank goodness, to respond to loving kindness; Laurie got the impression that that was a quality with which he had so far had little contact.

Stella watched those first days of Laurie's mild dictatorship with maternal anxiety. Once she contrived to be in the private lounge while the child had his supper. She noticed that Laurie dismissed the waiter, and that Richard was much intrigued by the pyramid of fish with a snow-cap, about which Laurie concocted a story that necessitated at various stages the demolishing and gobbling up of parts of the little mountain.

Stella had ventured to remonstrate. "It's grand to see him eat so much, but don't you think his supper should be kept very small? He goes to bed soon after six."

"Tonight," said Laurie, "he's going to walk out in the gardens and see the stars before bed. I believe it's hunger that awakens him around twelve every night. He's more likely to sleep right through the night if he turns in half an hour later really tired and nicely full. I think the bath at night makes him sweat too much, too; excessive sweating can't possibly be good for him. We'll try an earlier bath and just a cold wash before bed."

"Every child is bathed before bed."

"A warm bath in temperate countries induces sleep. Here, it doesn't—I've found that out from experience. If a bigger supper and no bath will help him to sleep right through the night we'll have won quite a victory."

The idea was half-successful on the first two nights and wholly so on the third. To Stella, who had deliberately forgotten everything she had ever learned about nursing, it seemed like a miracle. It was easy for Laurie, of course; she had all this stuff at her fingertips. But what a blessing that of all the professions she had decided to train in child care. What immense luck for herself and for Richard!

Laurie tried not to think too much about Stella, but once or twice the bitterness she had felt at their first meeting had been revived. There was the time she had dined rather early at her table for one in the hotel dining-room and was on her way out when Stella and Eduardo with two or three others were taking their places at the large, be-flowered table always reserved for them. Stella had gestured gracefully, displaying a deep, sapphire-encrusted bracelet, and looked at Laurie with the aloof charm of a countess.

"You have had a good dinner, Miss Bell?"

"Yes, thank you," Laurie had answered with a smile, and passed on.

The bad moment had come next day, when she was taking Richard to the shady fringe of the bay. Outside the hotel they had met Eduardo. He had greeted her with his usual courtesy, then said gently:

"Miss Bell, when we met you at dinner last night you were a little impolite to Senhora Alvares. Not wittingly, I am sure. I think it is that you do not quite comprehend our ways of addressing others. As you know, my wife is English and therefore reluctant to put you right in these matters; she would not wish to hurt your feelings. But you are too sensible to take it amiss if I ask you to please address her as senhora. She was not affronted, you understand?"

Hot cheeks averted, she replied, "I'm sorry, senhor. I'll remember."

The tiny incident spoiled several hours for Laurie, but it also served to harden the shell she was growing against such pinpricks. It would not be long, she consoled herself, before Stella and Eduardo would take off in their plane for the African mainland, and once they were gone the whole thing would be much easier to bear. She did wish, though, that before they set off some more homely abode could be found for herself and Richard.

And then almost, it seemed, by chance, a villa above the sea presented itself.

Laurie, trim in a grey linen skirt and a white blouse, was carrying Richard pic-a-back from the beach one morning when the amethyst and chromium car drew up on the Esplanada opposite the hotel and the tall, dark Marquez appeared from it and strode to meet them.

He bowed, said, "Good morning, Miss Bell," and immediately lifted Richard to the ground, adding severely, "I would say that you are wise for children but not for yourself."

"Richard isn't heavy."

"Heavy enough, when the sun is so high," he said with a shrug. He bent a charming smile upon the child. "So, Ricardo, you are to learn the clipped English like that of Miss Bell. But never," he stooped and wagged a forefinger, "must you call me that abominable word 'uncle.' Always Tio. *Compreender aquilo?*"

"Yes, Tio Felipe." Richard gave a sleepy smile and murmured, "I did want a carry. My legs is really tired."

"I take him early to the beach to avoid the worst of the heat," Laurie explained. "He'll rest in his room now, till lunch time."

Felipe swung the child into the crook of one arm. "Come, then, Miss Bell. I have something of importance to communicate to Senhora Alvares which will be of interest to you and to this godson of mine. To the lift!"

The porters stood stiffly to attention, and the Portuguese reception clerk bowed from the hips. Laurie felt as if she had inadvertently slipped into a royal procession, and savoured the novelty of it. Even the native lift-boy breathed an awed, "Senhor Marquez!" and hurriedly squeezed himself into the smallest possible space beside his push-buttons.

Felipe talked gaily to the child, and did not set him down till Anita had admitted them to the lounge. The servant curtsied and hastened away to her mistress. Felipe flicked open a crested gold case, selected an opulent-looking cigarette but did not light it. He stood looking through one of the doors to the balcony at the vivid coloring of growth, the beach and the ocean.

"You are finding Mondego to your taste, Miss Bell?" he enquired.

"Very much, thank you, senhor."

"You do not miss the harshness of the English climate?"

"Not yet."

"Ah, you make reservations. We have something here which does not please you. I wonder what it is?" Apparently this was intended as no more than a conversational gambit, for he strolled out to peer over the balcony, and did not come in again till Stella rustled into the lounge.

She was wearing another of those remarkable hostess gowns, in parchment silk this time, with tartan cuffs which accentuated the fineness of her white wrists. Felipe greeted her in his usual fashion as if she were the only woman in the world, releasing her hand with a faint air of reluctance which must have endeared him to many women. He knew all the tricks, this Felipe, thought Laurie, and possessed many morc of his own copyright, besides.

"A surprise call, Felipe," Stella said. "How very kind of you. Eduardo is out having a conference with our pilot." With a graceful movement she swooped to press her lips to Richard's temple. "Have you had fun, my darling? I think you have. Say good-bye to Tio and you may go with Miss Bell to your room."

Stella had not looked at Laurie. She seldom did when others were near. But Felipe's detaining hand as Laurie was about to obey the intimated command brought Stella's blue gaze round upon the small slim figure of her sister; a gaze which for the moment was carefully expressionless.

"I have come here upon a matter which concerns Miss Bell. I would like her to stay for a few minutes," he said. Without words, he indicated that he would prefer to see them seated, and waited till they were comfortable before continuing: "You have mentioned, Stella, how much it would please you to leave Miss Bell and Richard in a house when you start away on your tour. I have thought about this and I find I can offer you one at Villa Barreiro. It is normally occupied by my bailiff, but while I am in residence to keep an eye on the estate, he is going on leave to Lisbon. It would please me to have Richard so near to the Palacio."

"It would please us, too—immensely," said Stella, in her low, measured tones. "It's very sweet of you, Felipe."

He gave her a smile which would have made the heart of a more tender woman behave queerly. Laurie herself experienced an odd stab somewhere inside. "The sweetness is in your acceptance of the house," he said lightly. "The place is completely furnished and quite modern. There is also the old couple who are servants to the bailiff, so Miss Bell will be adequately chaperoned. I suggest in addition two native servants. A simple household."

Very simple, thought Laurie soberly. An improvement, anyway, on the present arrangement. She saw that Felipe was regarding her with some keenness and quickly assumed a polite and impassive smile, but before she could answer his unspoken query, Stella said:

"It will be such a relief to know that Richard will be quiet and well cared for. I think Eduardo and I will enjoy this tour of the plantations more than any we have made before." A pause. "Did you wish to say anything in particular about the plan to Miss Bell?"

He gave a careless shake of the head. "Only that she will be in charge of the house and may make any temporary alterations she wishes. The keys are already with the porter at the gates of the Palacio and can be collected at any time."

"I see." Stella nodded agreeably at Laurie. "Very well, Miss Bell."

Laurie held Richard's hand and went with him, through the door opened by Felipe, to his room. As usual, it took her several minutes to recover from Stella's remote graciousness, but presently she was able to take an almost excited pleasure in the prospect of living alone with Richard on the estate of the Marquez de Velho Barreiro. Stella and Eduardo would be away for a least two months, and during that time she, Laurie, could be natural with the child—and with herself. And what a boon that was going to be!

She peeled off Richard's expensive white suit and unstrapped his sandals, gave him a quick wash in the adjoining bathroom and popped him into his cot. When she turned back from drawing the curtains his eyes were already closed, and she paused there, looking at Stella's son and reflecting, a little wistfully, upon the unerring good fortune of her sister.

In the quietness she heard the voices of Felipe de Velho Barreiro and Stella Alvares. Her mind toyed with the possibility of Felipe being half in love with Stella; only half in love, because a man of his kind would never permit himself to fall wholly for a married woman. But what if it had been he and not Eduardo who had turned up at that hotel in Cannes? Wouldn't he have been bound to be captured, as Eduardo was? Felipe was now about thirty-two; he was practised alike in charm and generosity and his very aloofness suggested experience of women of the world.

Laurie gave herself a shake. She was as bad as the rest, going all breathless over the Portuguese nobleman. She had to get used to him as part of her life. He would always take an interest in Richard, and the child's parents were his nearest friends. At Villa Barreiro she was bound to meet him occasionally, and perhaps again and again she would have to suffer that overbearing kindness of his.

He treated Miss Bell differently from the way he treated other women. No cynical charm, none of the slightly dangerous compliments for Richard's nurse; merely that smothering, firm kindness which left one like a leaf in the wind, without a will of one's own. He was certainly accustomed to getting his own way.

Upon which reflections Laurie resolutely drove him from her thoughts.

CHAPTER THREE

IT WAS AT Stella's suggestion that Laurie paid a preliminary visit to the house at Villa Barreiro.

"You must decide upon Richard's bedroom," Stella said, "and make a note of your requirements. You can even take some of your own things along with you, if you like. It will save you trouble when you're packing."

"How do I get there?"

"By car, of course. Pedro will take you later this afternoon, and as I shan't need Anita you can leave Richard here with her. After all, you're entitled to a little time off whenever it can be managed."

Laurie excluded irony from her tone. "Thanks. Looking after one child isn't exhausting, and I have a rest when he does. But I would like to go to Villa Barreiro this afternoon. Will you tell the chaffeur?"

Stella nodded. "While we're away you must get into the habit of giving him plenty to do; previously he's had too much slack time. And, Laurie"—her voice lowered—"I've let it be known that you have my entire confidence. You're above the rest of the staff, in a category of your own. Eduardo agrees that that is how it should be."

Laurie said. "I am honored, senhora."

A slight smile widened Stella's lips, but she spoke with more than her usual earnestness. "You're taking it marvellously, Laurie, and I promise I'll make it up to you. All I ask is that you go on giving your very best to Richard."

"You know I'll do that."

Laurie did not linger for more conversation with Stella; she knew that her sister was as aware of what remained unspoken between them as she was, and nothing could be gained from repeated discussions.

During siesta the hotel assumed a deathly quiet, for even the waiters and messengers disappeared to their beds. The porters sat somnolent, one each side of the wide entrance, and it was rare indeed that they had to stir during the two hours following lunch.

At four, however, activity began to rustle through the corridors and lounges. Tea trays were delivered to bedrooms and suites, bath taps were set running and the whole atmosphere became brisk with the anticipation of a long cool evening after the day's glaring heat.

Laurie did not sleep in the afternoon. She mostly read, because it was too sticky for sewing or writing letters. Today she had a bath, drank her tea while she dried as thoroughly as possible, and got into a pale green frock which had only straps over the shoulders; the breeze over her skin was glorious. Having been assured by Anita that Richard would be carefully watched, Laurie went down to the waiting car, sank into its upholstery and told Pedro to make for Villa Barreiro.

She felt glad and expansive and wonderfully fresh. The coast road, part of which she had walked on that first day, opened out before them, a pink-tan ribbon between wild banana and nut trees. Here and there in a clearing showed a group of native huts; circular mud walls and conical thatches with sisal and agaves growing about them. Pigs and scrawny hens sought among nearby shrubs for sustenance, and women lazily pounded corn or lounged in the sun while naked children tumbled in the grass with an assortment of sharp-nosed kaffir dogs.

Soon, the luxuriant wildness on each hand gave way to orderly plantations of papaws, bananas and tea, and the tiny houses built on the European pattern were overflowing with Indian families; a door open here and there showed women in faded saris and brightly-dressed, dark-skinned children. Then these dwellings, too, came to an end, and the car entered Villa Barreiro, where white villas rested among mauve flowering Judas trees, wide-branched tamarisks and tall palms.

A quiet, flowery little town with a neat shopping centre and a quaint harbor which might have been transported from old Portugal itself, so worn were its walls and patched the sails which showed above them.

Villa Barreiro, Laurie had learned, was part of the de Velho Barreiro estate. The inhabitants worked in the profitable plantations and in the small factories which handled the sisal, the geranium essence, the cloves and the cotton. Each produce had its manager who was answerable only to the Marquez.

The car wound out of the town on a straight road lined with budding magnolias, and Laurie saw from quite a distance the tall pillars and great curly iron gates of the Palacio. Her heart turned with the beauty of those gates in such a setting. The gatehouse was just inside them to the left of the drive, a splendid, rambling building which gave a hint of the grandeur hidden back there among the trees.

Pedro stopped at the gates and gave a tug at the chain which operated a distant bell. A little Portuguese in a smart white uniform produced the keys for which Pedro asked and directed him to the Casa Margarita.

The car reversed, they sped back down that scented avenue and turned on to a road upon which houses were set at long intervals in large gardens. In front of one of these Pedro braked.

"This is the Casa, senhora. You wish me to go with you?"

"Just bring my suitcase, will you? Then you can wait for me in the car."

As Laurie first saw it, the Casa Margarita was a magic house. White and one-storied, a steep, green-tiled roof which reached down over a verandah that was nearly the size of a *pateo,* and white stone pillars twisted like sugar sticks. The garden was a riot of scarlet and flame with here and there the white and pink flowers of dark-leaved shrubs. The whole of it dreamed against a silken blue sky.

Laurie drew a deep breath, broke off a blossom and clipped it into the framework of her white bag. She opened the front door and found herself in a tiled lounge which was chiefly dove-grey and maroon with a flowered linen easy chair sedately set at each of the four corners. There were one or two pieces of carved furniture and a pair of lovely French vases, and on the wall hung a series of mezzotints.

Happily, she hurried through the rooms. The corner bedroom for Richard, she thought, loving the pale blue and gold; and the one next door for herself, so that they could both glimpse the sea. Except on humid days he could play in the paved verandah, though something would have to be done about the fountain. It looked like a miracle, playing out there in the slanting golden sunshine, but held a danger for a child.

Coming back into the lounge she sighed with pure pleasure. It was going to be just heavenly living here above the sea, with the wind pouring off the ocean into their bedrooms and no one to worry them. The couple of months ahead would make up for the grim disappointment of a week ago, and beyond then she refused to look.

She snicked undone the suitcase which Pedro had placed upon a chair and took from it the odd pieces her father had given her and the mementoes she had bought at the ports on the way from England; foolish little things, these last, but she was loath to part with any of them. Perhaps they should all be closed away in one of the cabinets for the present. She was about to gather them up when a long shadow preceded its owner through the doorway.

Laurie stood very still and her heart began unaccountably to beat rather harder than usual.

"Ah, there you are, Miss Bell." The alien tones, well-known now, were cordial. "I have heard that you came to the Palacio gates for the keys and thought I would come to bid you welcome to the Casa Margarita. Have you already made an inspection?"

"Yes, senhor."

"You like what you had seen?"

"It's a beautiful house." Her fingers were closed tightly round an ivory pin-box purchased in Mauritius. "Richard will be very happy here."

"And you," he said, "will you be a happy child, like Richard? I hope so," he added, as if what she might answer were unimportant. He looked about him. "It is modest but comfortable. I am inclined to agree with you, Miss Bell, that ordinary surroundings are necessary for the child."

"I haven't said that."

"No, but I have seen you bristle with that sentiment—and how demurely you have bristled!" His regard was quizzical as he stated. "You have an affection for Richard and a large-sized conscience, so you will do him much good. You look forward with pleasure to living in this house, do you not?"

"Yes, Senhor Marquez."

"Senhor, simply," he said. "You need no alterations here?"

"It's risky to have a fountain where there's a child. I'm afraid we'll have to keep it dry."

"Oh." He backed a pace and stared sideways through the window at the billowing golden rain. "You are right. I will have it done."

He looked back into the room, eyed her collection of possessions on the carved blackwood table and picked up one of them, to examine it critically. It was a small round box of hand-beaten metal; the pattern of flowers was punctured all over on both sides and the two halves fitted together so tightly that those long, sensitive fingers went white at the tips before he parted them. Inside the box was green with age and it smelled musky.

"A pomander box," he murmured, and looked at her. "Have you then some interest in such things?"

She smiled. "I do rather enjoy period pieces. I took a fancy to that box and was given it for my eighteenth birthday. It's one of my treasures. In a better light you can see the pattern very plainly and tiny rubies on both sides."

He turned it about. "I see them. Where did you get this, Miss Bell?"

"From my father. I wanted him to sell it, but he insisted on my having it."

"So you have a father," he said in the pleasant, slightly mocking tones which Laurie could not decide whether to like or hate. "Tell me about him.."

Her smile deepened a little and, unknown to her, her eyes glowed softly with all the love she had for Henry Fielding. "He's sweet and unpractical. He has a little shop in York where he sells all sorts of objects—old things like Victorian writing tables and copper ware. He buys up bronze and silver vases and turns them into reading lamps—I used to make the pleated silk shades for them. He could never afford to buy many real antiques, and when he did, of course, he just hated having to sell them. He'd absent-mindedly hide them." The glow in her eyes misted over. "Years ago, when he first opened, he called the shop 'Miscellany', and that name is still up, though much weathered."

"And you also had pleasure from his business?" asked Felipe. He nodded down at the box which still lay in his hand. "I have a somewhat similar one in gold which belonged to an ancestor of mine; it is in better condition but it is possibly the same age as this."

She gave a small laugh. "My father says that one is sixteenth century and was probably the property of a sailor because it's been knocked about and is just the size of an orange, and oranges were scarcely known in England then; a sailor might have got one in the Mediterranean. My father's quite positive is smells of the dried orange that travellers carried to ward off disease."

Felipe lifted his shoulders in his inimitable shrug. "Why should he not be right? This father of yours is a man of imagination, and I would say you must be much like him. Take your pomander box, or I shall steal it."

He helped her to stow her goods into a blackwood chest, locked it up and placed the key on her handbag. With a gentle tug he released the blossom she had tucked into the top of the bag, and gazed at it enigmatically.

"A white oleander. I think it is your flower, Miss Bell. It is innocent, of regular formation and very cool to the touch."

Laurie was aware of heat rising from her neck. What did he mean by that! Nothing, surely. He had not spoken in the manner he used with Stella; there had been a suggestion of satire. Yet he had flickered a glance over the pale skin of her shoulders and made her feel suddenly exposed.

He went on impersonally, "Have you noticed how mysterious is the heart of an oleander, Miss Bell? Innocence and mystery often go together, I think. One cannot know what will appear when the innocence is challenged, can one?"

Apparently he had a way of asking probing questions and avoiding their answers, for now he moved towards the door as if the session were at an end. Laurie took up her bag and the various keys. She would have liked to stay longer and inspect the kitchen and the servants' quarters, and it would be pleasant to wander in the garden now that the sun was well below the zenith and find out how big was this domain of which she was to be mistress. But that would have to wait till another day.

Before reaching the porch, however, Felipe paused and queried, "You have some knowledge of paintings, Miss Bell?"

"Not much. I've been to the galleries in London but I'm no critic."

"But you are willing to learn more?"

"Naturally."

With seeming irrelevance he asked, "When will you move into this villa?"

"On Monday," she told him. "Senhor and Senhora Alvares are leaving on Saturday."

"So? I would like you to bring Richard to the Palacio for lunch on Wednesday. I have heard from an English art dealer that he will be arriving in Mondego next Wednesday morning, and I am instructing him to call upon me as soon as he gets here. There is the chance that he may have something good, and if not he may still be informative. In any case, as he is a countryman of yours with a taste for *objets d'art*, you will doubtless find him interesting."

"I shall be pleased to come, senhor."

A smile moved the well-cut lips. "In Portuguese you would say, *'Obrigada; o prazer e meu.'* Can you not manage that?"

Laurie made a bright attempt and he laughed, briefly. "It is a marvel that you English speak at all. You are afraid to move the mouth. Your voice sounds like that of Senhora Alvares when she was learning Portuguese." He faced her with aloof friendliness. "It occurs to me that there is a likeness between you and the senhora."

Laurie was suddenly rigid. The color he had caused to rise now drained from her face and she swiftly averted it and drew back her shoulders.

Coldly, sharply she said, "You are mistaken, senhor. There is no likeness."

"Perhaps not." His eyes were hawklike and his tones had acquired the hardness of steel. "Possibly it is merely an Englishness. It is of no consequence."

But Laurie was too frightened to heed the complete change in his manner. She had allowed herself to become bewitched by his comradeliness into completely forgetting the implications of her promise to Stella. In those minutes, while Felipe stood obliterating the light from the doorway, his face dark and drawn with something approaching dislike, she saw the utter folly of permitting freedom to her emotions. What a blind idiot she was.

The Marquez was clever and observant. He also had the fastidious code of an ancient family. Stella's bargain with her sister, if he ever came to hear about it, would disgust him entirely. But he must never come to hear of it; that would ruin everything—his friendship with Eduardo and Stella, her father's newly-won content and her own position here . . . everything!

Her sinews tightened. He seemed to be waiting, with the courteous patience he would have extended to a stranger, for her to speak.

"I must go," she said. "It will soon be dark."

He pressed up the catch of the lock, motioned her to precede him and drew the door shut. He escorted her along the path and out to the car. As remote and chilling as a glacier, he opened the rear door.

"I trust you will soon feel at home in the Casa Margarita, Miss Bell," he said formally, with an air of utter indifference.

She was seated, the car door snapped into position and Pedro started the engine. She saw Felipe's bow and, without turning her head more than a fraction, watched him slide into the preposterously long and gleaming car with the crest on the front. A few seconds later he passed them at great speed, and not far ahead he swerved left, up the magnolia-lined avenue to the Palacio.

Only then did Laurie's breathing even out. She was trembling, and wishing fervently and futilely that the Marquez had stayed away from the villa. She didn't believe that he suspected he had hit upon anything approaching the truth, but the very fact of his spotting a similarity between herself and Stella, be it only a trifling inflection when she tried to pronounce Portuguese, showed that he was a difficult man to deceive. Thank heaven Stella would soon be going away. By the time the Alvares returned to Mondego the Marquez himself would no doubt be ready to leave.

Involuntarily, she recalled his face as he had walked down the path at her side. Tightened up and expressionless, forbidding her to remember that they had, for a few minutes, talked freely and naturally as man and woman.

She could not help wondering what he was thinking as he drove between those great pillars towards his palatial home. Perhaps he was reflecting that it had been foolish to invite the English girl to lunch. Richard could easily have been brought and returned by one of his own servants. Well, he could send a polite cancellation if he wanted to. But she did hope he wouldn't—at least, she thought she did.

By the time she arrived at Porto Mondego, Laurie's nerves were almost ragged, and the white flower she had been clutching as they left the Casa Margarita was in shreds on the floor of the car.

The feverishness preceding Stella's departure worked up to a crescendo. The jewels were locked away in their special travelling cases and placed in the care of the hotel detective till the last moment. The plane was tested hourly and the meteorological charts watched as if anything less than perfect flying weather would be an affront to the wealthy Alvares.

No wonder Richard had become delicate, thought Laurie. What an atmosphere for a child! As much as she could she kept both him and herself away from the private suite, but towards evening on Friday, Stella called Laurie to the lounge.

As usual, the Senhora Alvares was exquisitely gowned. She wore an ice-blue cocktail suit which by contrast softened her eyes, and a set of diamonds and pearls at her throat and in the lobes of her ears. The ash-blonde hair had the polished sleekness inseparable from Stella, her facial make-up was flawless, and her hands nearer perfection than a film star's.

"We're having a small farewell party tonight," she said quietly. "They'll all be up here to cocktails, but we shall dine downstairs. After Richard has had his supper I want you to bring him in for a few minutes. Eduardo likes to exhibit him occasionally."

"Very well," said Laurie. "Do you wish me to come with him—or Anita?"

"Bring him yourself. You needn't dress—they won't expect it of you."

The slight snub sounded deliberate. Knowing that Stella was more keyed up than she appeared, Laurie made no comment. She waited.

Stella took a cigarette from one of the massive jade boxes and tapped it on a long pink fingernail. She spoke moderately, but very clearly. "Why didn't you tell me when you returned from the Casa Margarita the other day that you met Felipe de Velho Barreiro there?"

"Was it necessary?" Laurie met her glance squarely. "He gave me no message for you."

"I have a right to know these things, and you are unable to judge whether it is necessary or not. Pedro heard you talking in the house for some time."

"Knowing the Marquez, you must also know that his chief concern was whether Richard would be happy at Villa Barreiro."

Stella drew on the cigarette, narrowed her eyes against the smoke and looked back at Laurie. "I suppose you're not so different from the rest of the girls here. They're all crazy about Felipe and he behaves identically with each of them. He's polite and maybe even a little teasing, but they mean nothing to him whatever. So don't flatter yourself that when he addresses you he's picking you out for attention. That's his way."

The sudden fright of the other evening still fresh in her mind, Laurie carefully kept all feeling from her voice. "I thought he might be like that," she said.

"The ingenuous type bores him," Stella added, "and the fact that he's half English rather complicates his character. Normally, the Portuguese don't care for their women to be too highly educated; they admire the domestic virtues. Felipe isn't quite like that. He likes a woman of experience, one who will accept his compliments as he means them, and lead him on in a sophisticated fashion. The young are apt to misconstrue."

"I can assure you he doesn't pay compliments to me."

"He wouldn't, of course," Stella stated with cruel carelessness. "I'm merely warning you not to worship the hero because it won't pay; you'd get nothing whatever out of it. Also"—a thin wire threaded her tones—"it will do you no good to count on his friendship. He's promised to keep an eye on Richard, so you'll see him frequently, but don't try to be anything that you're not."

"Don't worry," she answered. "I'm a poor actress."

Stella was apparently satisfied. She smiled, took another pull at the cigarette and squashed it out in a large silver ashtray. "Have you heard of Corina Queira?"

"Isn't she the young widow who lives in the big house at the other end of the Esplanada?"

"She is. Her husband died after only four months of marriage; it was all very sad and she was swamped with sympathy at the time. The men rave about her beauty—and she's certainly nice-looking," conceded Stella, who knew herself to possess looks which were more than nice. "That's the woman whom Felipe will probably marry."

Against her will Laurie asked, "How old is she?"

"About twenty-six. Highly intelligent, I believe, and keen to be more than the usual Portuguese wife. Her husband was a clever surgeon in Portugal and her father is the Conde de Garda—quite a big noise in Lisbon. After her husband's death she came here for a rest. That was two years ago, and it has become noticeable that she and Felipe invariably happen to be in Mondego—and elsewhere—at the same time. She was his companion at the races, just before you came."

On the point of making further enquiries, Laurie hesitated. This was a matter about which she could not afford to care; the private life of Felipe de Velho Barreiro could not impinge upon that of Laurie Fielding. She had to ignore whatever she heard about him.

"It's surprising that he isn't married already," she said offhandedly.

Stella smiled down at those slender hands of which she was so proud; a shrewd, secret smile. "The more a man sees of the world the more difficult he is to please; you'll learn that as you grow older—particularly if you stay on with us. Felipe is complex and he needs the kind of woman who could understand his complexities. In fact, he needs all women in one. I should say that Corina is the nearest he's likely to get to his ideal. She's knowledgeable and really elegant."

Eduardo came into the lounge then, and Laurie slipped along to Richard's room. Bathing the child, she forgot the brief conversation with Stella. She ordered his supper to be served in her own room, a change which awoke Richard from his usual evening languor. Between eating spoonfuls of creamy omelette he chattered about all the exciting things they would do next week, after Mama and Papa were gone. He seemed actually to be looking forward to their departure.

Though he had been in her care only a short while, Richard had swiftly formed the habit of turning to Laurie for everything. She was what he had needed; a companion and playmate, someone who would listen to his half-intelligible monologues and teach him rhymes without being impatient when the words eluded him. And now he strutted when he had victoriously brought out the final devastating word to every line of a favorite verse.

In his childish way he had come to realize that nothing was too much trouble for Laurie. He could demand whatever he liked of her and monopolize her, which was something he had never had a chance to do with Mama. She made up stories about the big, colored pictures in his books, and gave him rides on the great furry dog on wheels which he had never called anything, but which Laurie had named Woofie. Woofie, through Laurie's imagination, had acquired a picturesque family background and a large personality. Richard was beginning to find his little world exhilarating.

The telephone at her bedside rang, It was Stella, the gracious employer.

"Richard can come along now, Miss Bell. Ten minutes —no longer."

The crowded private lounge reeked of expensive cigarettes and perfumes. Dark, beautifully-gowned women spoke to Richard in their own tongue, sounding honeyed and loving; they kissed his forehead and stroked his skin. The men patted the curly head and paid jovial compliments to Eduardo. Stella stood aloof, a drink in her hand, smiling in the consciousness of her son's fine features and good behavior.

When she reached Stella, Laurie lifted the child. "Say good night to Mama," she said.

Stella bestowed a light kiss on each of his cheeks, Portuguese fashion. "Good night, darling boy. Have a lovely sleep." And then: "You may take him now, Miss Bell. Good night."

"Good night, senhora."

A group of guests parted to give her access to the door. It was opened for her. Laurie passed through to the corridor and with a tiny shock looked up into the tanned face of Felipe. In a flash she thought of Stella, watching the half-open door, and the smile which rose unbidden to her lips was instantly frozen.

"I'm sorry I didn't bring Richard to you in the lounge," she said abruptly. "I didn't see you." You ought to have seen him, prodded her heart; he's head and shoulders above every other man, in every way.

Flipe bowed coolly. "I have only this moment arrived. I saw you leaving and thought I, too, must bid good night to Richard." He spoke to the child, then looked at Laurie. "You are displeased about something, senhorita?"

"No," she replied quickly. "Of course not.'

"What is it then?"

"Nothing, I assure you."

"It does not irk you," he asked with strange, cold persistence, "that you are unable to join such a party as this one, here?"

"No, senhor." She had the horrid sensation that Stella was coming nearer, that at any moment she would be sent about her duties; which would be insuportable in front of Felipe. "Please excuse me. I have to get Richard to bed.'

Perhaps that was the wrong way to address a marquez; Laurie was too agitated by the approach of Stella to care. She saw his thin nostrils dilate slightly and the narrowing of his eyes. His bow had no warmth; it was the automatic gesture of custom.

"I shall expect you and Richard for lunch next Wednesday, as we arranged. *Adeus* to you both."

He moved away and the door closed.

Richard said, "You're hurting me, Laurie," and she swiftly loosened the fingers she had unconsciously tightened about his hand.

As she went quietly about the business of getting him to bed her mind was dominated by a word of four syllables. Felipe had called her "senhorita," and she found herself liking it a great deal better than "Miss Bell."

CHAPTER FOUR

STELLA and Eduardo went off next morning, emitting showers of reiterated instructions. At the smallest sign of ill-health in Richard, Laurie must consult Dr. Lopez. She was to write regularly to the addresses already in her possession, and they would be satisfied with nothing less than a full weekly report.

It was easy, Laurie discovered, to agree to whatever they demanded, and the moment when she and the child watched the plane fade into the silver haze was one of utter relief. For many weeks ahead her life was to be her own and Richard's; for the greater part of the time she could forget Stella.

She slept in the large bedroom of the suite that night and the next, and on Monday morning Pedro loaded the luggage compartment of the car and drove Laurie and Richard to the Casa Margarita.

For Laurie, the day of settling in was filled with the happiness of anticipation. She met Sofia and Giulo, the leathery old pair who ran the house for Felipe's bailiff, and chose two native boys, one to do the laundry and the other to polish the expanses of tiles and parquet and to keep the kitchen supplied with fuel.

The fountain, she noticed, was dry and clean and a new padlock secured the faucet; Felipe had kept his word. The garden was long and walled in by acacias and scarlet-flowering gums which shut out the houses to right and left. From the back there sloped upwards a thickly-wooded hill which, Sofia explained, had occasionally to be combed for destructive monkeys. Not much else lived there, though.

Sofia was an excellent cook but so awed at having to cater for the Marquez's own godson that she was privately glad when Laurie made it known that she herself would prepare the child's food. They collaborated in the kitchen, just as Laurie joined forces with Giulio in the garden.

The old Portuguese were a couple to delight the heart of an English girl who had never before had contact with Latin people. Sofia, in her long black skirt, cotton blouse and striped apron, with straw slippers upon her feet and a white mob-cap over her greying hair, was a figure from an old print; and Giulo's faded beret with white curls standing up around it, and loose trousers drawn in at the ankles, were part of the lovely old harbor and waterfront which could be seen from the corner window.

The splendor of the Hotel Carmac and the sophistication of the shops on the esplanade had seemed out of place on an African island; Laurie had appreciated them yet felt vaguely let down. Villa Barreiro, on the other hand, merged restfully into the lush greenness of Mondego. Some parts of the town, Laurie guessed, must be quite ancient. The cobbled streets close to the waterfront were narrow and twisting, but many of the houses there had fine baroque porches and ornate grilles to the windows. The upper balconies were discreet affairs from which the women of a family could see without disclosing themselves.

Sofia knew and loved the history of Villa Barreiro. In painstaking English which she had picked up while a young maid at the Palacio to the old Marqueza, she answered Laurie's queries.

"It was a Barreiro who discovered Mondego during the time of Prince Henry the Navigator, " she declared with pride, "and for reward he was given half of the island; the other half was government property but was sold gradually to private landowners. The Barreiro estates in Portugal are in the south and the west, and they cover thousands of acres, but always the family have loved Mondego. It is said that the old Marqueza was happier here than in Portugal."

"You mean the mother of the present Marquez? Has she been dead long?"

"Two — three years. She died in England." Sofia's manner as she said this was as vague as if England were a legendary country; as indeed it must be, to her. "She would drive about the island in a smart black equippage which had the Barreiro coat-of-arms on the side, and when we had a *festa*—we of the staff of the Palacio—she would be alight with jewels, and would dance, too, when she was younger. She was so far above us, yet one of us at those times. Every one of us respected her and loved her. It will be good," she stated reflectively," when there is again a Marqueza. They say it is possible the Marquez would have his marriage in Mondego. He would be the first Barreiro to do that, and it would make us very proud."

This being a subject Laurie had no inclination to pursue, she merely smiled and went from the kitchen down a wide corridor which had a window at each end. One of those windows faced Africa; it had a dial set in the ledge with a pointer permanently set to the northwest—towards Portugal, Laurie supposed.

Straightway, Laurie learned that life on this side of the island revolved around the Palacio, particularly when the Marquez was in residence. For no explicable reason she was reluctant to learn details about the Palacio itself, nor did she now look forward with any degree of pleasurable excitement to Wednesday's visit. Richard, though, was almost palpitating with joy when Laurie lifted him from his morning rest on that day and began to get him ready for lunch with Tio Felipe.

"Will I see the fishes, Laurie?" he demanded urgently. "Gold ones, red ones, green ones, all sorts of ones. Will Tio Felipe give me some fishes one day?" And so on, while Laurie patiently strapped his shoes and cleaned his fingernails.

By the time he was slick in a powder blue suit and had had his curls brushed back, Laurie had an impression of the Palacio as a huge aquarium. When Pedro drove between those tall, sculptured pillars a little later, however, she forgot Richard's babble in a breathless wonder. For the avenue itself was a winding, sun-splashed tunnel of beauty. There were tamarisks and yellow-garbed acacias, magnolias blossoming and wantonly dripping their surplus petals upon the statuettes which were set with delightful inconsequence at each side of the drive. And at the base of each statuette freesias sprouted, much bigger blooms, than Laurie had known in England.

The trees thinned to give a view of Manueline towers against the hot blue sky, and then the car was moving between formal gardens with high box hedges which here and there were clipped into arches and steeples, and in a moment or two had come to a halt in the Palacio courtyard.

Laurie had no time to stare at the massive exterior which had been fashioned in the golden days of the seventeenth century, for Felipe had come from the cavernous entrance, had opened the car door and, with a light hand at her elbow, was helping her on to the extravagantly tiled forecourt.

The coolness of marble flooring and fluted pillars was soothing; the extravagance of space and workmanship utilized by the baroque staircase which rose from the other side of the hall was breathtaking.

"Fish," Richard piped up tenaciously. "Want to see the fishes, Tio Felipe."

"So you shall, my little Ricardo." He turned to a uniformed servant and spoke in Portuguese. "Diniz, take the child to the fountains for a quarter of an hour. Watch him carefully and keep him out of the sun." His glance followed them to the terrace and he said to Laurie. "He is attracted by water and the things which live in it, but do not worry; Diniz will guard him faithfully."

For something to say, she asked, "What are these fish he talks about so much?"

A shrug. "Tropical species. You may care to see them yourself later. I should explain that I have been informed that our art dealer will be a little late. His ship put in at Porto only an hour ago, and he has to attend to the usual formalities. While we wait for him we will have a drink. This way, if you please, senhorita."

At the final word she looked up at him almost gratefully, but was unprepared for the cool amusement in his dark eyes—what color were they . . . a deep brown flecked with jet? She thought he had sensed in her an awkwardness in being thus left alone with him, and knew a faint prickle of vexation. How boundlessly sure of himself he was; how arrogant, with his beastly great palace, his hordes of servants and glorious wide lands under the African sun. After all, whatever his possessions, he was only a man!

As if she had sent out a thought line he said, "You will like the Palacio better when you have seen more of it. Possibly you English do not care for the exuberance of Manueline architecture; it is not every one's taste, but here it is somewhat offset by more severe interior furnishing." He was leading her into a long room which showed no signs of the severity he had mentioned; the atmosphere was aesthetic and beautiful. "Sit here, near the window, and we will have a chat over a long, cool drink."

He did not enquire what she would prefer, but gave her a pale topaz liquid in a crystal tumbler; it had the dry sparkle of champagne and even some of its headiness, but it was, he explained, a product of his own vineyards in Portugal, and fairly harmless; most women liked it. His own glass had a deeper hue.

He hitched his trousers and sat in one of the straight-backed, satin-seated chairs, and the thin gold case flicked open.

"You will smoke?"

"No thank you."

"You have never smoked?"

"A few times, but it isn't a good habit when one has the care of children."

He smiled and set a flame to the tip of his cigarette. In one economical movement the lighter was slipped back into his pocket and the cigarette taken from his lips. "You are very serious about this work of yours, are you not? Rather too serious, I think, for one who has not yet seen much of life. I told Senhora Alvares that you were too young for so much responsibility, but she assured me that you were older than you appear. At twenty it is wrong to be old."

"Looking after a child like Richard is by no means ageing," she retorted quietly. "He's almost too docile."

"I also thought that, but already he improves," Felipe answered. "I would not like to think that the improvement must be entirely at your expense, though. *Meninas* should have fun."

"*Meninas?*"

"Girls," he translated. "Young ladies like you." He sipped his drink and addressed her with a half-smile. "You pity Portuguese girls, do you not? You seldom see them without a duenna, and you feel their lives must be exceedingly dull and horribly confined. You do not know the half of it! They are full of happy intrigue, those girls, because they have not lost the knack of believing in romance."

"Girls everywhere are romantic," she said quickly, and stopped.

"No," he told her decisively, "they are not. In some countries they are so engrossed in this business of following a career that they lose the ability to recognize simple rapture. There are exceptions, of course, even among the English. The Senhora Alvares may have been one."

Felipe wouldn't know how ruthlessly Stella had carved the career she now followed, thought Laurie a little grimly. Without meaning to, she said, I suppose your own mother was another?"

His thick black brows rose with faint surprise at what must seem to him like a frontal attack. "Yes, she was." He tapped away ash. "Romance was very much alive when she was young, and she was naturally of the merry heart, also; one of your rare gay English women." His expression was soft and reminiscent, and as he went on his tones became attractively more and more alien. "Let me tell you about her. Her name was Marian, but my father always called her Mariana. She was an only child of wealthy Victorian parents and they lived in a big house in the Cotswold Hills. When my father was at Cambrdge he liked to spend his holidays at the house of one of his friends who lived also among those little English hills. My father and Marian fell in love and were married within two months of meeting."

"And were they happy?"

"Ideally." His glance held mocking enquiry. "In your opinion they should have been longer acquainted before taking the irrevocable vows . . . is it not? You are cautious, or perhaps an ice maiden where the emotions are concerned. Yes, I believe you are an ice maiden—that would account for your strange little withdrawals—but one day you will have to melt, because even the English have hearts which sometimes become unruly. I know that you have never yet been even remotely in love; therefore it is difficult for you to comprehend the passions of otheres. I assure you, though, that they exist!"

Although it was not many minutes since Laurie had asserted to herself that he was only a man, she had never until this moment genuinely regarded him as anything but a Portuguese aristocrat incapable, from some obscure cause, of ordinary reactions. She had imagined that he was probably capable of cool anger—had even had some small experience of his displeasure—but somehow she had seen him as too aloof to be completely human.

Now, she was less sure. This Felipe, who seemed to be testing the rim of a deliciously dangerous intimacy, was nearer in type to the man who had ordered her into his car on her first morning in Mondego. Then she had not known him to be the Marquez, nor had he realized that she was an employee of his friend, Eduardo Alvares. They had been just a man and a woman who had met in unconventional circumstances.

She smiled and tasted her drink, as if the comment she was about to make were of no consequence. "I should not have thought you were the kind of man to believe in love at first sight, senhor."

"No?" His mouth had the quizzical slant. "How else can love begin but at first sight? Two people meet and there is a difference in the atmosphere—a warmth, a pulsing which was not there before, the perilous suggestion of a promise. Perhaps all this is not very marked at the start, but presently comes the undeniable magnetism of one for the other, and to complete the story only background is necessary: a heavy moon and the perfume of a garden."

In his own fashion he was laughing at her, and the knowledge brought to Laurie a sense of release. This man was not such easy tinder to the flames of passion as he would have her believe; she was sure of that. He knew her to be young and untried, and he was rallying her, perhaps with the idea of making her face the reality of white-hot emotions, but more likely for his own private fun.

"You omit the guitar, senhor," she said demurely. "Sofia tells me that no Portuguese love scene is complete without the throbbing of a guitar."

"Sofia is not quite right. The guitar is merely an incitement employed by young men who are not too sure that their love is returned; it is also a form of compliment." Airily he snapped his fingers. "Me, I am not partial to the guitar. In a true love scene it would be a nuisance!"

Laurie laughed a little and leaned back in her chair. The last shred of her resentment fell away. This was so much better than she had anticipated. Felipe natural and amusing was an even more charming person than the man who kissed Stella's wrist and probably looked into Stella's and other women's eyes. She did not know that Felipe—did not want to know him.

"Now we have worked off this stiffness," he said, "you will have a cigarette. I insist.' '

He need not have insisted. Laurie, just then, had no wish but to please him. She took the cigarette, held it to his lighter and felt the impersonal brush of his hand upon her fingers. She caught a faint male fragrance and knew that her heart beat faster than usual. This was what Stella had warned her against—this feeling of delight and sweet compulsion in Felipe's company; every woman felt it and was momentarily swayed.

She spoke casually. "I've been told that here in the Palacio you have the finest *azulejos* on the island. I should like to see them."

"They are in the wall of the back terrace. I will show you them later. There is also a Moorish bath which I have had converted into a bathing pool, and a Moorish pavilion which is now among trees planted by my grandparents. The ceiling of the pavilion is particularly good, though there is a bigger one of the same type in the Castelo Barreiro, in Portugal, where I spend most of the year. There, at the Castelo, we have *azulejos* which are very amusing. Undoubtedly they are the work of someone who had an abnormal sense of humor, but he was an artist, too."

Felipe was again the urbane host, talking as politely as if she were a tourist. Had she yet seen the sugar factory or the Trappist monastery? She must not miss the remarkable view from the hill behind the Casa Margarita of the native reserve—many square miles of undulating countryside dotted all over with huts, each family group palisaded and surrounded by a tall crop of Indian corn. The land was their own, for ever, and gradually they were being educated to love it and serve it well.

Through the window she saw Richard in the distance, returning slowly with his hand in that of the short and stalwart Diniz. And at the same time she heard a car draw up in the courtyard.

"Ah, that will be the taxi of our friend the art dealer," said Felipe. "Do not disturb yourself, Miss Bell. I will bring him in here."

Left alone, she cast an interested glance around the salon. By palace standards it was small, and she wondered whether Felipe had used it deliberately, in order that she should not be overawed. The furnishings were an exquisite blend of fine carving and old-rose satin; a couple of landscapes hung on one wall and on the opposite side of the room a long mirror was framed in delicately wrought bronze. The chandeliers were magnificent. Laurie could visualize them glittering with light, sending out stabs of blue flame. There were fitted bookcases full of tooled leather imprinted in gilt, and fine figurines inside an old and beautiful cabinet.

Did he entertain much? What was the use of this splendid place otherwise? How strange it must be to live here alone, as he did, to know oneself the overlord of Villa Barreiro, to be courted and looked up to, and to be credited with super-human qualities. True, his responsibilities did not appear to weigh him down; rather they were part of him and, oddly, only a small part. He managed the town and his estate with an ease which sprang from heredity. Impossible to imagine him in any other sphere.

Was he conscious of his power over women? Yes, he must be. A man of his knowledge and experience could have no doubts about his effect upon the volatile emotions of his own countrywomen, but apparently he was moved by it only to gentle mockery.

Her reflections were cut short by the reopening of the door. Because she was also expecting Richard to come in at any minute, Laurie got up and took a few steps towards Felipe and his other guest. Only a few steps, though, before she knew the impact of sickening shock and had to stand very still.

The man with Felipe was young and fairish and above middle height. He was square-jawed and had a pleasant, crooked smile which lit up with recognition.

"Why, Laurie! I didn't expect to run into you so soon. And here, of all places!" He took her quivering hand in both of his, shook it warmly and hung on to it it as if to reassure himself that she was real. "Laurie, it's wonderful."

Felipe's voice broke in, very dry and even. "So you and Miss Bell are already acquainted. How interesting. You have known each other for long?"

The other man's debonair blue eyes widened slightly. Laurie's grey glance at him was dark with a silent, anguished pleading. She quickly withdrew her hand and spoke hurriedly, confusedly.

"Cedric and I were friends in England. He had dealings . . . business dealings with my father. He . . . I didn't think for a moment that he would turn out to be your art dealer. It's so amazing that I can't take it it in. You see. .. . ." She stopped, petrified by the implications of the situation.

Cedric Maybury here in Mondego—worse, here in the Palacio! What if he said something to upset the whole of Stella's scheme? Supposing. . . .

Her instinct clutched at a straw. Cedric was fond of her; he had put it into words more than once. He was decent, but a trifle unstable. Still, he did look as if he understood how imperative it was that he should be discreet. To be absolutely sure of him she needed to be alone with him for just a few seconds.

But Felipe was eying him with a deadly frankness, appraising him and finding him, if the compression of the well-defined mouth were any guide, somewhat less of a person than he had anticipated. The same dissecting gaze was bent upon Laurie, and she lowered her lashes and averted her head. What a ghastly position to be in!

Felipe's composure had hardened, but nothing could shake his infallible courtesy. "What will you drink, Mr. Maybury? I recommend a fine Madeira." He lifted a decanter and spoke coolly over his shoulder to Richard's nurse. "Miss Bell, I hear the child. No doubt he will need to wash his hands. Diniz will show you a bathroom."

Nails curled tightly into her palms, she threw one more desperate look at Cedric Maybury, who knew that she was Laurie Fielding, and almost ran out to attend to her nephew.

CHAPTER FIVE

LAURIE tasted nothing at lunch. She ate some of the jellied soup and tried the colorful salad with strips of tender white meat, but nothing had any flavor. Even the prepared fruits were no more delicious than chilled water on a hot day. Outwardly she gave most of her attention to Richard, but her mind registered every word exchanged between the two men, one of whom sat at the head of the table while the other was opposite.

Cedric, in the agreeable drawl she remembered, regretted that there had not been time between his arrival and the luncheon appointment in which to unpack the pictures he had brought, but he would be glad to wait upon the Marquez at his convenience.

"Come tomorrow, my friend," Felipe said, "and we will go into this business at once. You say you have the work of two new artists. Nothing old?"

"I've one beauty, which I think will appeal to you. A Tintoretto."

"So?" Felipe was alert. "Do you need to travel as far as Mondego with such works in order to sell them? I would say that even in present-day Europe there are people willing to pay much for a Tintoretto."

"Possibly," Cedric conceded disarmingly. "To be honest, I didn't try Europe. I came here because I'd heard about your collection and knew about your reputation as a patron of art, and also because," he put almost as much gallantry into the compliment as a Portuguese, "Laurie's father had told me she was here."

"I see." Felipe paused meditatively. "You did not know Miss Bell had left England?"

"Well, no. I hadn't travelled north for some time. I'm now with a new firm in London, and mostly have to stay on the job." With some of the aplomb Laurie recalled, Cedric changed the subject. "They tell me that moist heat has a devastating effect on some canvasses. What has been your experience, Senhor Marquez?"

The conversation slid into technical channels, and at length, to Laurie's relief, the meal ended. Politely Felipe shepherded them from the gold and grey dining-room and out into the wide, tiled terrace. They took a leisurely walk in the shade of tall trees and palms, down through sloping gardens gay with color, in and out among exquisite statutory and arbours, round pools covered with fat, exotic lilies, and banked with tropical ferns, up hewn steps to where the big, domed pavilion stood white in a sylvan setting.

Felipe must have forgotten his half-promise to show Laurie the pavilion ceiling, for he passed the building with a wave of his hand. He talked charmingly of who had planned this particular garden or that, and he shouldered Richard and teased him about the fish.

They came back to the Palacio through formal gardens with balustrades, and mounted to the back terrace, which was walled with blue and white *azulejos* representing old shipping scenes. A schooner was painted on the ceiling, black and grey picked out in gilt on a very blue sea.

Here in the terrace Laurie was able to forget for a while the peril represented by Cedric Maybury. How she wished her father could see these *azulejos* of galleys and allegorical personages. He'd revel in this place; the beautiful floor tiling, the orate ceilings, the cloisters, the cupolas, and the mixture of Gothic and Manueline architecture. How reverently he would linger over the lovely old furniture and peer into the portraits.

Impulsively, she turned to Felipe. "You didn't show us the Moorish swimming bath."

His expression had become remote, almost stony. "It is too hot for more walking and I am sure you have seen seen enough for one day. Perhaps some other time."

"Siesta time," said Cedric cheerfully. "We English never seem to get the hang of it, so you must forgive us. May I call a cab from here, sir?"

Stung by the tone Felipe had used, Laurie swiftly readjusted her wits. Before the Marquez could offer the use of one of his own cars she said lightly, "You can go in our car, Cedric. After Pedro has dropped us at the Casa Margarita he'll take you on to Porto. Besides, I want to ask you about my father."

They walked round the terrace to the forecourt. As if conjured by telepathy, the biege car rolled up to the Palacio entrance and Pedro got out. But it was Felipe who opened the car door and saw Laurie seated, with Stella's beige cushion in the small of her back. He did it impersonally but with his usual dignity; the *cavalheiro* speeding his guests.

"Tomorrow at ten," he said in English to Cedric. Then he stood back from the car. *"Adeus!"*

The car ran around the drive and down the avenue towards the gates, slid between the pillars and out on to the road. Cedric pushed a hand through his thick, light-colored hair, let out a sigh and grinned at Laurie.

"Good Lord, what a man,' he said. "Charm, and a dagger at the hip."

Swiftly, she nodded to indicate Pedro, and placed a finger to her lips. Cedric made a sign of comprehension and sat back in his corner regarding her with the same smile she had always thought was one of the pleasantest she had ever come across. He was being wonderfully accommodating.

It was about three years since she had first encountered Cedric Maybury. He had come into her father's shop on a Saturday morning when she happened to be there, and somehow, because he knew a great deal about reconditioning antiques, he had gone home with her father and herself to lunch, and spent the rest of the day with them.

After that, whenever she had a week-end off Cedric turned up and they played tennis or went to a film together. He was good-looking in a rugged way, and blithe; he always had plans for enjoyment, and his enthusiasm for a gay life was infectious, a tonic she needed after a spell of hard work. He even made love as if it were a game and Laurie had parried him in a similar vein.

Then, quite unexpectedly, had come the offer of a post in London. After light-heartedly thinking it over Cedric had accepted, and had left behind a flock of promises. During the following weeks he had written her a cheerful letter or two, but other things, such as coming to Mondego to be nurse to Stella's child, had begun by then to fill her mind, and if she had thought of him at all it was with the half-pleasure one derives from looking back over happy times in happy company.

Since arriving on the island she had not once thought of Cedric Maybury, and had it been suggested that he might show up on this very island in the Indian Ocean she would have laughed her unbelief. Yet here he was!

Away from the Palacio she was able to think more clearly. She simply must have a talk with him, but how to explain her position was beyond her imagination. To tell him the complete truth would be to beg for trouble. Cedric did not know Stella, and like most gay people he was capable of exploding with indignation. His loyalties could not help but be with Laurie and Henry Fielding.

"When did you see my father?" she enquired a little desperately.

"About ten days ago—I travelled to Cairo by air. He sent you lots of messages, and I promised to see him when I get back to report about the set-up here." He winked reassuringly.

"Is he well?"

"He's fine." He looked down at Richard, who sat between them but, to Laurie's relief, forbore to make the remark which must have been hovering in his mind. "Nice-looking youngster," he commented, "but a bit on the slim side."

"He's going to grow up into a handsome *fidalgo,*" she said and managed, with a beseeching little smile, to convey a desire to talk no more for the present.

At the Casa Margarita, Pedro opened the car door. Laurie got out and said casually, "Will you come in for an English cup of tea, Mr. Maybury?"

"This trip has been an eye-opener for me," he said. "I thought all tropical houses were of mud with tin roofs and that they were overgrown by jungle and falling apart with ants. As for the Palacio . . ." he shook his head. "The Marquez de Velho Barreiro must be rolling in it."

Sofia had not yet risen from siesta; the house was cool and quiet. Richard had gone drowsy, so Laurie put him in the striped canvas swing which was just outside the french door on the verandah, secured the strap about him and came back to face Cedric.

She smiled at him and gave a hopeless little lift to her shoulders. "I can't tell you the truth and I don't want to tell a lie. So what am I to do?'

He came nearer, laughed down at her in the light, caressing way he had. "Just say you're glad to see me. None of the rest matters very much."

"I would be glad if I weren't worried."

"This is the first time a woman ever worried over me. I like it." He took her hand and squeezed it. "Seriously, Laurie, I won't give you away; you know that. But I'll admit I'm intrigued. What's all this 'Miss Bell' business?"

She bit on her lip, hesitating. How she loathed being committed to tell all this subterfuge and deception. "It's just an arrangement I made with someone. There's no intrigue, but I gave my word to be known here as 'Miss Bell.' I couldn't possibly forsee that you'd turn up!"

"No, my sweet, you couldn't. Where's your sister?"

"Please!" It seemed to Laurie that the very shadows were straining to listen. She answered him softly, urgently. "I haven't a sister. I'm nurse to Richard Alvares, and the Senhora Alvares is my employer. You see, Cedric. . . ."

"I believe I do see—part of it, anyway.' The nonchalant smile had sharpened, and he pushed his hands into the pockets of his out-of-place tweeds. "The rich senhora didn't want a sister—but she was in need of a nurse. Don't deny it—the pretty flush convicts you both. What a fool you are, Laurie!"

Still quivering, unwittingly, from Felipe's reprimand, Laurie felt that she could tolerate very little from Cedric. Yet she knew that handled correctly he need constitute no menace. She had to be patient, and very friendly.

"You make it appear dreadfully important, and it isn't," she told him. "It has no importance for anyone else. Just remember I'm Laurie Bell, that's all."

"I'd like to tell the Senhora what I think of her!"

"You won't be able to. She's gone away for two months." She managed a laugh, but it was not so steady as she would have liked. "You're taking this like an affronted hero. How do you know I'm not doing it for personal gain?"

"Because I'm darned sure you never in your life did anything with that end in view," he retorted. "If anyone's going to gain from this masquerade it won't be you. It would serve you right," he added with unwonted sternness, "if something happened to make you regret taking such an idiotic step."

"Such as what?"

"Such as . . . well, falling in love under a false name. Ever thought of that?"

"No," she said slowly, "I can't say I have."

"Not that I'd care to have you fall for a Portuguese—but that's what you deserve! I've never heard of anything so crazy in my life."

"My father mustn't know," she said. "It's between you and me, Cedric. And please don't ask any more questions, because I can't betray anything told me in confidence."

He shook his head. "I'm in a maze—quite winded, and it's so damned hot that I can't think."

"Then give it up," she suggested. "Forget all about it and sit down. You have a bit of explaining to do yourself."

He dragged one of the easies nearer to Laurie's chair, knocking a rug askew on the mosaic floor as he did so. Sofia would disapprove of that; indeed, this young man would find disfavor in any Portuguese household. His manners, the senhoras would declare, were altogether too free, and dull gold hair in a man was not to be trusted. They would forgive the weakness of his mouth, might even be partly vanquished by the ready smile, but to them comradeliness was a quality to be indulged only among men.

"How do you happen to be travelling around selling paintings?" she demanded. "I thought it was supposed to take years to learn about such things, and a few months ago you knew no more about them than I do."

He gave her his easy grin. "If you have the nerve you can get away with anything in this world—and by that I don't mean anything personal! You probably remember that I joined the London firm as a glorified patcher-up of antiques? They're biggish people and keep a couple of travellers who, I discovered, make fabulous commissions on sales. So I was keen to get out of the workshop and do a bit of travelling myself. I tried in England and sold a couple of pieces and a picture or two, and then the Tintoretto came in—fortunately while the other travellers were away. The boss said it would have to be sold abroad—at a staggering figure, by the way. If I pull it off the commission will equal six months' salary, and my expenses are paid, too. So you can imagine how keen I am to get rid of it."

"Good heavens," she said soberly. "Is it worth so much? Weren't you terrified that it might get smashed on the journey?"

"It's crated and was well taken care of. I shall unpack it this evening."

"What made you go up and see my father?"

"I felt I would rather have his suggestions about the type of people to contact than those of my boss. Your father knows so much. He gave me some advice and we naturally got to talking about you. When he told me you'd cleared off to Africa I was furious. You hadn't even sent me a good-bye note."

"But I hadn't seen you for weeks and we were too far apart to go on being friends. I was quite sure you understood that."

"I see," he said with chagrin. "One has to be ever-present to rate a place in your affections. We used to have good times, though, Laurie."

"Very good times," she agreed, "and please don't think I wasn't grateful. I missed you a lot at the beginning, but guessed you were taken up with new people."

"Too many," he acknowledged ruefully. "If you're to get a kick out of life, London's expensive, and I just couldn't afford a week-end trip to York. Sometimes I'm sorry I made the change. I've never met another girl like you, Laurie."

"I'll accept that as a compliment," she said. "Tell me how you came to hear about the Marquez. It's odd to think that he's known in England."

"Ah, the Marquez." Cedric kissed the tips of his fingers in what he conceived to be a continental gesture. "There's a man for you. Six feet of virility, wealthy, handsome, fascinating—and I believe he's even popular among men. He's well known through the trade as a buyer of rare things, though art dealers usually visit him at one of his Portuguese mansions. I found out that he was in Mondego and chose him to be the first on my list—because of you, my pet." He threw off business as he always discarded the unpleasant or uninteresting. "Is it possible to be merry in this little corner of red hell?"

Laurie's heart lightened. She recalled Felipe's words: "*Meninas* should have fun," and found that she agreed with them. Because she had charge of Richard life need not be monotonous, particularly while Cedric was here. She saw herself dancing while he sang nonsense into her ear; it was so long since he had done that.

"How long are you staying?" she asked.

"Two or three weeks, if I have luck. I'm supposed to get rid of all the pictures, but I haven't much hope of disposing of the new artists' stuff to your Marquez. He doesn't strike me as a man who'd look at anything priced under a thousand guineas—which is excellent in one way and grim in another. If he turns me down flat I daren't hang on long."

"I wonder. . . ." She had been going to mention the possibility of Sofia arranging a small party at the Casa, but the old woman herself came in then through the door which led to the kitchen. Sofia had been baking this morning and the smell of new maize bread drifted in with her.

Laurie made an introduction. Cedric, knowing what was expected of him but unversed in the Portuguese brand of politeness, nevertheless contrived a credible bow.

"I'm happy to know you, senhora." He sniffed with enjoyment. "That's a marvellous aroma you bring with you. I could eat a hot roll."

"What is a roll, senhor?" she enquired, rather sourly. Obviously, he should not have been alone with the young senhora, and she was not to be won by blandishments.

"A *paozinho,*" Laurie elucidated hastily. "Mr. Maybury came on this morning's boat to Porto. He's an old friend of mine.'

"Even so," pronounced Sofia, her face lined and yellow in the afternoon light, "he should observe our customs. However, a friend of the senhora is welcome. You wish some tea, Miss Bell?"

"Yes, please, Sofia, and Richard's small glass of milk —I'll get the lactose myself."

Sofia went out, leaving the door wide as if to remind the Englishman that protection for Laurie was not far away.

"Cheerful soul," he remearked. "The type to get joy from the sadness in life. I suppose her greatest happiness is in pessimism.'

"She lives in the past, when Villa Barreiro was a feudal village. She was born here, which means that she's ingrained with a reverence for the *grande senhor* and all he stands for. I find her refreshing.

"I should say she's tiring," he said. He gave her a long and curious stare. "What in the world has happened to you, Laurie? Aren't you bored living here alone with an anaemic child and hemmed in by that tough, crumpled old woman? It's a fantastic way for an English girl to live, and I wouldn't have believed it of you if I hadn't seen it myself."

"Women like to be hemmed in. Didn't you know that?"

"Only by their own husbands and children; certainly not by a bunch of Portuguese. You'll never stick this— you can't." As he leaned towards her his regard was lazy but sincere. "If I sell the picture will you go home with me? We couldn't marry yet, but we could be engaged and make plans."

She raised her brows in mock surprise. "A proposal, Cedric? How astoundingly naive, coming from you."

"The odd thing is, I mean it. I'm thirty and it's time I did something really worthwhile; marrying you would certainly be in that category." A notion came to him and he said, suddenly eager, "I might put the commission on the picture into your father's business and help him expand. You always liked the shop, Laurie, and we could be happy there."

"You're ignoring the most vital aspect," she said. "We're not in love."

Nor, she admitted to herself, had she the least wish to go back to York. She would like to see her father, of course, but all the old, familiar things seemed fantastically far away and shrouded in unreality. Only the present was real; this house and the brilliant garden out there beyond the veranda, Richard, Sofia, Giulo and all the somnolent beauty of Villa Barreiro. She couldn't leave them—not yet.

"I love you," he answered, rather doggedly and out of character.

"Are you trying to persuade me or yourself?" She smiled at him. "Let's leave it—because I'm quite sure that when you've made the acquaintance of one or two senhoritas you'll change your ideas. They're beautiful, and much more responsive than English girls."

"I can imagine that, if each of them is dogged by a duenna!"

"That's the thrill of it. They talk with their eyes and red lips—no one can express so much without words as a Portuguese girl. Even the peasants do most of their courting with a gate between them, except at *festa* time. Life is so simple here!"

The whisper of Sofia's straw slippers announced the tea tray. Cedric got up at once to take it from the gnarled hands, and he bent upon the old servant his most winning smile.

"So you brought the *paozinhos,* senhora!" His abominable accent conjured a tight-lipped response to his smile. "Golden-brown rolls, primrose yellow butter and pink cakes with cherries on top. What a colorful feast. Portuguese women must be superb housewives."

"The best in the world," Sofia told him decisively. "Even here in Mondego where we have no wheat flour and butter only from tins we make many good things."

Heat had withered the flesh from Sofia's bones, cyclones had toughened her moral fibre and the sun had thickened her skin into crinkled parchment, but she was fiercely of the opinion that no other part of the world—not even Portugal—was so well worth living in.

Cedric stayed another hour, and when he left he promised to let her know Felipe's verdict upon the Tintoretto. He looked into Laurie's grey eyes and at the slim shoulders clad in sunflower silk.

"You stand out among these people," he said. "Quiet, fair-skinned and lovely—and infinitely restful. The best of you is that you don't change in this tilting world." A grin. "I'm getting sentimental, Laurie. Prepare yourself, darling. I'm going to kiss you."

But he didn't, because Laurie stepped into the porch, and just along the verandah Richard paused in the pastime of jumping up and down in the swing in order to watch events. So Cedric departed wearing a wry smile.

Laurie lifted Richard from the swing and took him indoors. She was tired. How quickly the day had passed, yet how long it seemed since she had dreaded the visit to the Palacio. That was over now, thank heaven, but something else had popped up to exercise her brain.

Her first frantic disquiet over Cedric's arrival in Mondego had smothed out into a background of uneasiness which was bound to last as long as he remained on the island. Yet part of her was glad to have him near, at least for a time. He was English and ordinary, not charming at one minute and hostile the next. His ways were easy-going and calculable. Yet his presence here was a danger she could not afford to neglect.

For her own peace of mind she ought to see him often, which was a state of affairs that Sofia would oppose. Sophisticated types of enjoyment existed in Porto Mondego: the Casino adjoining the hotel, dancing in the Carnac ballroom beach suppers and moonlight bathing. But Laurie was tied to Villa Barreiro; indeed she was always within call of the Casa itself after Richard was in bed. How to have fun with Cedric was a problem.

Next day, however, she was offered enlightment.

CHAPTER SIX

LAURIE was in the garden just after noon the following day when a girl of about twenty-two came in at the gate and walked with a springy step across the lawn. She was dark-haired and olive-complexioned, with the typical rich red lips and brown, sparkling eyes of the young Portuguese.

"*Bom dia!*" she cried, with the exuberance of one young senhora greeting another. "I am Isabel Gourros. We live not at the next house but the next."

Laurie was on her feet and happily indicating the deck chairs in the shade., "I'm glad to know you. I expect you've heard that my name is Laurie Bell.' The surname came glibly now; it had to. "Won't you sit down?"

"There is not time. I must go straight back for the *almoco*—the lunch, you say. My mother would have called but she has not much English and you are without a guardian. You must know that the mothers always address themselves to each other. She sends me instead, to ask that you will come to a little party we are giving tomorrow for my brother's birthday."

"How very kind. I'd love to come."

"Also," Isabel pressed on, "we wish to invite the English senhor who is your friend.' She gave a whole-hearted chuckle. "It amazes you that we know about the Senhor Inglez . . . yes? Here, nothing is secret. The servants talk, and so do we. It makes life!"

"It certainly did . Laurie told herself she must be doubly careful. "At what time is the party?" she asked.

"You will come when the small senhor is asleep, *hà?* Sofia will watch him for the evening. We will say seven o'clock. You yourself will ask the Englishman?"

"Yes, I'll send him a note by chauffeur this afternoon. I'm sure he'll be delighted to come.'

"*Bem!* What is he called?"

"Cedric Maybury."

Isabel repeated the name with a comical rolling of R's. "It is a droll name, that. I have never yet met an Englishman. He will be an experience." She paused. "I must warn you that my brother has already seen you in the garden and near the beach and admired you very much. He is twenty-six tomorrow, and the shipping agent for the Marquez. *Adeus,* Laur-rie!"

With a vivacious wave of the hand she was out on the path in the hot sunshine, and a few seconds later she pulled shut the gate and disappeared. It was as if a flame had blown into the garden and withdrawn without consuming anything.

Laurie knew during the rest of that day and the early part of the one following that what she had needed was a social event to look forward to. This was her first and she meant to make the most of it. Fortunately, too, Sofia was benignly in favor of her attending the Gourros' party, though she did mention, somewhat tartly, that Senhor Maybury would feel out of place at such a gathering. There were already more young men than young women in Villa Barreiro, and the English senhor, according to Sofia, had been invited only because that bold Isabel had thought it might be exciting to make his acquaintance; she was always wanting something new, that girl. Laurie was privately of opinion that Cedric, once he had recovered from his initial aversion to the Portuguese temperament, would give Isabel all and more than she expected.

She waited till Richard was in bed before she took a bath and got into the green organdie. Oddly, her reflection was not so pleasing as she had anticipated, perhaps because there stole upon her a sensation of impending disaster; it was foolish, but unquestionable.

Cedric turned up before she was ready and the noise of his arrival kept Richard awake, so that she had to beg Cedric to go on without her and make her apologies. She would be along as soon as possible.

"I wanted to talk to you before we go," he protested.

"I'm sorry, but you'll have to wait till later," she said. "I can't leave till Richard is asleep, and with the windows wide he can hear everything. If you stay he'll never drop off. Please go, Cedric, and I'll follow."

He mumbled something about the child being a pest, but went out. Laurie sat quietly in the lounge, turning the pages of a magazine. Because she could not settle to reading a story the minutes dragged and she began to wish she were not going out. Cedric had looked disgruntled, for some other reason, she thought, than that she would not accompany him to the Gourros'. Probably the heat was getting him down; having travelled most of the way by air he would notice it more than she had.

Sofia crept in and spoke in a loud whisper. "The child sleeps now. You must go or Almeido will be next to arrive to escort you."

Almeido, Laurie had learned, was the brother of Isabel whose party it was. She drew a white chiffon scarf about her shoulders. "You'll call me if Richard wakens?"

The old woman nodded. "Go along now and have the good time. I will be here."

"I'll look in later."

Another tolerant nod. "I cannot forbid you to do that, but it will not be necessary."

Laurie flitted out into the night. She went out of the gate and along the gravelled road with its wide, clipped edging of grass in front of the garden walls. The next house was in darkness, but the next, the Gourros', blazed with light and lanterns hung in the trees and illuminated the crowded *pateo*. But before she reached the gate Laurie almost stopped.

Cars were parked on the opposite side of the road where turf sloped out to the rocks, but close to the gate stood a huge, bronze-colored car which, though she had not seen it before, she knew could belong to only one person. For, apart from its opulence, there was an enamel and silver crest placed centrally at the top of the gleaming radiator; a coat-of-arms she remembered, the only one ever seen in Villa Barreiro.

The interior of the car was softly lit, so that it was not difficult to see that the driver's seat was empty. In the back sat one of the grandees whom Laurie knew by sight as a friend of Eduardo and Felipe, and beside him was his wife. Next to the driver's seat another woman was snugly ensconced; a beautiful creature with slightly waving, silky black hair which was drawn back into a knot, and a pale, clever face which had the high cheekbones and thinnish nose of the Portuguese aristocracy; Laurie was beginning to know the types of features very well. The regal head rose from a collar of stiff white quilted silk.

Felipe was here, but not to stay. He had probably called in to congratulate Almeido, after which he would be on his way . . . with Dona Corina Queira. Laurie moved on, into the shadow of an arch laden with bougainvillea. She heard the slow ending of a fado, the liquid sorrow from Almeido's throat, the moment's dead silence after the final note had faded, and then Felipe's voice, mocking and with a smile in it, as though he had enjoyed the tragic singing with his tongue in his cheek.

"Almeido, my friend, you are in song. Tonight you will capture the hearts, but I implore you to be gentle with them; some hearts are brittle!"

The rest of what he said was drowned in laughter and clapping and cries of *"Outra vez, Almeido!"*

How long she stood there Laurie could not have said. She must still have been straining intently towards the *pateo,* for she did not hear steps on the path and she started violently when a tall figure confronted her.

He drew a brief, surprising breath. "My faith! I thought it was a pale green ghost." He peered closer. "You are white, senhorita. Is something wrong?"

Her voice seemed to come in a whisper from a long way off. "No, there's nothing wrong, thank you, senhor. I had to be a little late because Richard took longer than usual to go to sleep."

He did not ask after Richard, as she had expected. Instead, he stood looking down at her, coolly, speculatively. "You have seen Maybury this evening?"

"Only for a few seconds. We had no conversation."

"Oh." He paused for quite a long moment. "You are certainly disturbed and I wish to know the cause."

Suddenly, unreasonably, she could bear no more of him. Let him go to the woman who awaited him! "If I'm disturbed you must be the cause, senhor. I'm not accustomed to having my moods questioned and analyzed."

"I see," very quietly. "You resent my interest?"

"If it were genuine interest," she answered above the heavier, accelerated beat of her heart, "there would be nothing to resent. Will you excuse me?"

The fact that he ignored her final request was ominous in a man to whom gallantry was second nature. "When you do speak with Maybury later this evening," he said in a voice of steel," he will tell you that I have forbidden him to pay long visits to you at the Casa Margarita. I have heard that he remained with you for two hours after you left the Palacio the other day. In England such things may be permitted, but in Mondego they are certainly not done. You understand, Miss Bell?"

"You've forbidden him?" she echoed, the chill of fear in her tone; fear of what might happen if Cedric had to seek his pleasures elsewhere. Then before she could think clearly: "How dare you do that!"

His face visibly darkened and the nostrils drew in. "I think you sometimes forget you are living in Villa Barreiro."

"No one ever lets me forget," she cast back at him bitterly recklessly. "You least of all. I thought it was a kind gesture on your part to allow Richard and me to occupy the Casa, but I'm beginning to realize it was nothing of the sort. You wanted Richard close enough to be under your supervision, and because I'm only his nurse, I must toe the line, like . . . like one of your employees. You expect me to conform, to be as obsequious as the rest of these people who are under your thumb. . . ."

"Enough!"

He blazed. His hand came up to grip her arm just below the shoulder. She felt it hard over the bone, pressing as if with a twist of his fingers he would snap it. What had she said? What would he do now?

The heavy beat of her heart had turned into a queer, hysterical rhythm. She didn't care what he might do. Let him say what he liked; hurt her, if it would please him. That was what he wanted to do—*hurt!* It was in the electric ferocity of his grip, in that quick, violent breathing.

The cool and mocking senhor was roused, was capable, she knew in that instant, of a passionate and ruthless cruelty.

Eyes huge and dark with nightmarish thoughts, she stared up at the angular outline of his face, waiting tensely for whatever might come.

It was he, of course, who recovered first. His hand dropped, and pushed in an unaccustomed manner into his pocket. He took a short step backward and gave her an almost jerky bow.

"I beg your pardon, Miss Bell; I am afraid that for the first time in many years I lost my temper. However, I do not forgive you for using such words to me; they were insulting and unnecessary. I repeat that I will not have indiscretions committed on Barreiro property. If you and this man Maybury are . . . lovers, you will conduct your little affair with propriety. I advise that you get it over quickly and let him go. He does not strike me as the type to have much use for a faithful heart." Another bow, more suave and remote this time. "Run along to your party, child. Good night."

Laurie passed him, moved under the flowery archway and up the path to the *pateo*. Even when she was being formally presented to the Gourros' parents and Almeido a little later, she still quivered from those shattering minutes with Felipe.

There was very little about Almeido's party that Laurie remembered afterwards. The general pattern of it was already familiar through Sofia; the laughter and drinking of wine in the *pateo,* the tables in the verandah loaded with dishes of egg-cakes and sweetmeats, olives and fruit, and many finely-shredded salads. There were trays of almonds, walnuts, raisins and figs, small cream moulds topped with minced nuts and cherries, and round red cheese from Portugal which had had to remain in a refrigerator till the last moment.

At nine, and again at half-past ten, Laurie went to the Casa to see if Richard were still sleeping, and each time she was accompanied by the attentive Almeido. He was a pleasant young man who every one said would make a big success of his life. No one had been surprised when, on the retirement of Nuno Ferreira, the Marquez had appointed Almeido Gourros as his shipping agent. True, he was young, but he had been educated in Lisbon and he had the business mind.

He also had a mind for other things, Laurie discovererd. His voice was soft and persuasive both in speech and in song, and it was not his fault if she did not rise to the murmured compliments and the ardent glances; he accomplished them superbly. Tonight she was too numbed and miserable to care whether or not she had an admirer.

It was late before she had a word alone with Cedric. A big circle had formed for a country dance, and Laurie stood well back, watching as the couples twirled into the centre of the ring. Cedric came to her side, dabbing at his neck with a handkerchief.

"Indefatigable, aren't they?" he said in a brooding voice. "I suppose they re-charge during siesta. Is there somewhere we can sit where the lights are not too strong?"

They found an old green-painted seat, he waited till she was comfortable and then sank down beside her with a groan and leaned his arms forward, along his thighs.

"So this is a Portuguese binge! My feet are twice their normal size and I'm full of wine, Isabel Gourros is a machine which never runs down.'

"You owe her your invitation here tonight."

"I guessed that. She's a delicious piece that I'd have enjoyed at any other time, but just now she has no appeal. She's totally without sympathy and I'm worn flat."

"This is Portuguese Africa," she said. "I wonder if British Africa is anything like it?"

"Probably not. We take England into our colonies, but not the England of folk-dancing and village festivals. Portugal itself is very hot in summer, so the tropics to them are just a little warmer. They're good colonists because wherever they go they take with them their simplest pleasures as well as their sophisticated ones. Imagine finding an ancient castle tenanted by an English peer in the heart of Nigeria!"

Laurie was silent for a bit. The conversation must inevitably come round to Felipe, but she didn't want it to—not yet."

"Nigeria is a new country," she said. "The Portuguese islands have been settled for three hundred years."

"And the Portuguese nobility are outlandishly rich," he added. "They can afford to run estates in several countries. Also," he said, sitting up straight and savagely digging his heel into the path. "they can be as overbearing as they like, and we poor worms have to put up with it because we're dependent on their generosity."

It had to come, thought Laurie hollowly. Cedric meant to share his grievance, and in a way she didn't blame him. It must be humiliating for a man to have to put up with the arrogance of another man. It was bad enough for herself.

"Wasn't the Marquez interested in the Tintoretto?" she queried.

"No." He seemed unable to relax, which was unusual for Cedric. He pulled an ankle up on to his other knee and held on to it while he stared moodily at the gay scene not twenty yards away. "He didn't turn it down; merely said he was disappointed. I couldn't understand it. The canvas is very big and full of color, and the figures are excellent. It isn't unlike a Tintoretto he showed me in his gallery." Cedric gave an exasperated sigh. "He made me look closely at his own Tintoretto and, honestly, I couldn't see that it was better than mine. But he was glacial from the start and only looked at the stuff I'd brought out of politeness, and how polite that man can be!"

"I'm sorry. It's the dickens of a way to come for nothing.'

He smiled at her briefly. "Not for nothing, Laurie. You're here, and I'd never have been able to come if the supercilious Marquez hadn't been here, too. But it's disheartening, because I'd counted on his not being able to resist La Gioconda herself if he'd a mind to."

"What are you going to do?"

"I don't know. I haven't been able to think about it."

"Couldn't you try some of the other people in Porto Mondego?"

"I have sold one of the new ones for a hundred pounds —which means just ten pounds for me, lucky dog." His sigh was tinged with bitterness. "The Tintoretto is big money. In Mondego there's only the Marquez who'd pay such cash for a work of art. I wish," he looked at her with humorous resignation, "that I had the ear of the good-looker he's supposed to be going to marry!"

Laurie's nerves jumped and her teeth went tightly together. For several heartbeats she felt quite sick. Then she forced herself to raise her head and speak casually.

"You mean the Senhora Queira? How on earth did you manage to hear that rumor so soon?"

He nodded negligently at the dancers. "Isabel whispered it while the great Felipe was listening to her brother's throbbing tenor. He doesn't strike me as a man in the throes, but apparently every one here is sure he's in love with Dona Corina. I'll bet that if she asked him to buy the picture he'd fork out like a lamb."

"Don't you believe it," she said in a hard little voice. "Felipe is always the master, never the slave. No one could persuade him to do anything against his will."

"Still, a woman who'd fallen for his face and fortune would be bound to have a good try, and if she liked the picture so much he'd give it to her; he's the sort to hand out lavish presents. Once I had the cheque I wouldn't care what happened to the canvas." He shook his head regretfully. "You used to be my luck piece, Laurie. When I lived up in York I often had small slices of good fortune, but in London my luck was out. D'you know, I was convinced that if I came to Mondego you'd turn the tide for me."

Laurie did not answer this. She was realizing the truth of his first remark. Yes, Felipe would give anything to the woman he loved; exquisite jewels, rare and beautiful *objets d'art*—so why not the Tintoretto? It would, of course, have to be hung in his own gallery once tney were married, but Laurie had no difficulty in imagining the mixture of teasing and tenderness with which he would display it.

"I tell Corina that this is not one of Tintoretto's best—the greatest masters have had their failures!—but she says she must have it. So what would you? It seems the Barreiro gallery must contain one folly!"

It was uncanny, the ease with which she could visualize him and hear those alien, attractive tones. She could even be sure of the words he would use and the way he would speak the woman's name: caressingly, but with a slight emphasis on the final syllable.

Laurie shivered and dragged her mind back to this moment and Cedric. "Wasn't there," she asked, "some other unpleasantness between you and the Marquez?"

Cedric laughed shortly. "Mondego is like a percolator, isn't it? Every drop of information drains through. I didn't intend you to know that."

"He told me himself this evning. I was annoyed."

He mistook the cause of her vexation. "That was nice of you, Laurie. But we do have to keep on his right side, don't we? I fell a bit down about the way he's practically ignored my stuff, but I haven't given up hope; it doesn't do in this job. I won't come to the Casa Margarita any more than is necessary. We can meet elsewhere and try to find some spot where we shan't be continually spied upon. Now that I know these Gourros people I can call here, too."

"It really has been good to see you, Cedric, but . . . well, don't you think it would be wiser to pass on to the next art fancier on your list?"

"No," he answered flatly. "For one thing, there isn't another of the Marquez's standing, and also I refuse to leave this dubious paradise till you and I have some sort of an understanding. Don't forget that you're half the reason I came, Laurie—more than half."

"We've been over that!"

He turned to her with a grin. "And we shall go over it again, my sweet, till you're tired of saying no. The salesman is good at wearing-down tactics you know. In any case," he finished practically, "I've been allowed several weeks in which to unload my wares and I'm not the type of idiot to rush back to the grind before I'm expected. When I'm accustomed to the heat I shall begin to enjoy myself."

Laurie was too depleted to argue. The Alvares's tour of their plantations had hardly got under way, so there was plenty of time before she need become really anxious.

All parties have to come to an end, and the one at the Gourros' residence terminated with a final burst of song at midnight. Twenty minutes later Laurie was in her bed and staring out at the soft dark sky. She was weary but wide awake and more than vaguely unhappy.

She recalled the sudden flare of Felipe's anger and his contemptuous comment about Cedric: "He does not strike me as the type to have much use for a faithful heart." And inevitably upon this came the picture of Corina Queria, her head poised above the tall white collar, her face lovely in composure. It was like Felipe to fall in love with a woman who semed so eminently suitable in every way. He would make a tempestuous lover, but the tempestuousness would be schooled by that iron code of his. Had Corina the "faithful heart?"

Conjecture in the night invariably complicates and enlarges a problem. By the time Laurie slept Stella had returned to find Cedric broadcasting the fact that Senhora Alvares and Richard's nurse were sisters, Felipe was married, and even the child had withdrawn from Laurie his confiding affection.

CHAPTER SEVEN

DURING THE following couple of weeks Laurie drifted along quietly in the Casa Margarita. Once or twice she went to tea with neighbors, and one morning Isabel and several of her friends called in for a gossip and a cup of chocolate. It was pleasant to have women to talk to, but so few of them knew any English that half what they said passed her by.

Every other day a chauffeur from the Palacio called to enquire after Richard's well-being. "The compliments of the Senhor Marquez," he would say, "and how is the little *menino* this morning?"

Laurie would tell him: "Richard is well and sends his love to Tio Felipe."

"The senhora also is well?"

"As you see," she would answer with a nod, and wish she dared ask whether the Marquez had specifically instructed him to make this last enquiry.

Cedric was fast making friends in Porto Mondego among people connected with others who might purchase a picture or order some piece of period furniture which he knew his firm to have in stock. Laurie gathered that he was getting to grips with the climate and becoming as popular with the young Portuguese as he had been with the young English of London and elsewhere. He sent her a note:

"To get to know these people you have to play with them at all hours of the day and night, and I'm only hoping my efforts will pay dividends. I do wish you would come into Porto, Laurie. You have the car and it's easy for you. The two taxis here seem to be free only when I'm booked up. It's such a grisly waste, to be so near each other yet unable to meet, and—as I've told you before—you're such a restful person, darling, that I'm just longing to be with you."

Laurie was uncertain how to reply. Would he sail away the sooner if she saw him often? It was hateful to long for him to go; he had given her so many happy times in England and even paid her the compliment of proposing to her, yet she was aware that she could know no real peace till he had given his word that he would keep her secret, and departed.

She felt safest plodding through the days at the Casa Margarita, and there was a happiness in it, too, for Richard thrived as she had known he would, given the chance. The diet she had worked out for him had eliminated the bouts of sickness to which he had been subject. Because she regulated his day to make him healthily tired, he slept his full quota every night, and consequently the languor was disappearing and his cheeks taking a tinge of pink. His brain became more lively, and he quickly picked up all the small things she taught him.

His skin texture was like Stella's and slow to tan, but Laurie persevered; she would love his little body to be brown and lithe. She paddled with him in sea pools and dipped him in the ocean when she bathed. Watching him plop a stone in the water or chuckle with joy when a wave washed over his shoulders, she would smile on the lump in her throat and resist the urge to scoop him into her arms and bury her lips in his cool, firm flesh.

Stella should have known that what the child most needed was his own home and a great deal of love; ordinary, maternal love, not the smothering fondness of a mother who took a fierce, possessive pride in him.

To Richard, life was becoming more and more absorbing. In the garden he did important jobs with his toy lorry and trailer, and on the beach he found it vitally necessary to match one periwinkle shell with another or to find a piece of sponge which was free of anemone weed and coral. He and Laurie gravely discussed his business and decided all the steps to be taken.

He was not yet of an age to seek friends. So long as Laurie could be called upon to assist, admire and give counsel, Richard was happy. He brought her his little successes, took to her also the small disappointments and sadnesses which cloud every little life, and showed her how brave he could be when he hurt himself.

There came an afternoon, however, when the demands upon his courage were overwhelming. After his rest Laurie had taken him to the harbor, and for a while they had watched native boys converting a huge mahogany log from the forest into a fine, watertight boat. Each boy worked with a primitive chisel which he tapped with a stone, but there was little uneveness about the result of their labor. The log was being hollowed out smoothly and efficiently, and the interior of the boat took the classic shape while the boys sang an accompaniment to their activities.

Soon Richard tired of the sight. He wandered along to his favorite tiny lagoon and Laurie, perforce, followed him closely. She saw him standing with the calm water about his ankles, intently examining a bright flat stone which he held in his wet, sandy fingers.

Suddenly he gave a nerve-wrenching scream and toppled. Almost before he had reached the sand she was on him and had swept him up, but he was kicking frenziedly and letting out those terrible yells with all the breath in his lungs. It was all she could do to hold him.

"I've got you, darling," she panted. "What is it? Tell Laurie!"

It was about two minutes, though it seemed nearer two hours, before she caught the strangled words, "It's *burning,* Laurie . . . my legs!"

Swiftly, she sat down and examined him. Her face went pale and frightened and she had to frown and close her eyes against his screaming and take a hold on herself as well as on him, before she could look again. Both ankles were a swollen scarlet with purple weals about them; one was puffed to twice its normal size, the skin shiny and stretched as if it were ready to crack.

She couldn't believe it Only five minutes ago she had looked at his feet lapped about by cool water and thought how sturdy his legs were growing. Now they were an appalling sight. Were there such things as sudden fevers which attacked the limbs in this way? Could this be a poison of some kind showing itself? She knew that anything could happen in the tropics.

She leapt up, clasping him tightly in her arms,. and began the hot, slithering climb up the deserted slope towards the Casa.

By the time she reached the road her breath was coming in long, excrutiating gulps and her brain was crazed. Her heart hammered madly in her chest and throat. Someone ran down from a house and she managed to croak, "Will you go on and send Pedro for Dr. Lopez?"

It was twenty minutes before Dr. Lopez turned up, and during that time Richard only ceased his dreadful weeping to take breath for more. Sofia was terrified. In her years on the island she had heard of this but never seen it. The "devilfish" some called it. Ah, the poor *pequeno*. He would surely choke to death with the crying before they could get the doctor here.

Laurie scarcely heeded her. She wrapped Richard closely in his cot, leaving his feet free. To the ankles she applied a compress of ice water, and as she changed it and soothed back his hair with a cold damp cloth she whispered anything which came to her tongue in the soft, level tones he knew so well.

Before the doctor arrived Pedro came in.

"Senhora," he said, "I also took the liberty of going to the Palacio. I thought you would wish that the Senhor Marquez be informed."

"The senhor?" she echoed mechanically. Yes, of course! Felipe would know what to do; he would have met this before. Her eyes glazed with thankfulness. "You were right to call at the Palacio. Is he coming?"

"No, senhora. I am told that the Senhor Marquez is out for the evening."

"Oh." It was as if she were alone again in a cold wind. "Thank you, Pedro."

Then came the doctor. He was middle-aged and comforting. He gave the child an injection, had a good look at the ankles and smiled encouragingly at Laurie.

"You did your best, *meninal.* It is a terrible sensation, this sting, even for an adult who has learnt to endure pain. To a child it is insupportable."

"A sting?" she asked faintly.

"We call it that because we are not really sure how the thing works. The sting-ray is a small jellified fish which has a long blue string attached to it. Sometimes this string is two feet long, and it is full of poison. The fish buries itself just under the surface of the sand while the tide is out, but the string is left exposed. If it is trodden on it will instantly twine itself about the foot or ankle."

"We've never come across one before."

"They are not common here—you may never see one again. The little Richard was unfortunate."

"Isn't it . . . serious?"

"Not physically. The swelling will subside during the night as the poison disperses, but the pain may be intense for as long as three hours, which you will know as you are a nurse, can cause shock in the young system. The injection will lessen the pain and help him to sleep. Do not disturb him in any way, not even to undress him. I will call again tomorrow." He looked at her hair, streaked with sweat, at her worn face and at the scratches on her arms. "You are a good nurse but you must know that it is unwise to suffer with the patient. You, too, have had a shock, and I would prescribe the common remedy—a warm bath and then to bed. The child will not cause much more fuss tonight."

She saw him out and wished him good night.

It was dark, now, and Richard still cried, though with less violence. Laurie stayed near his cot till sleep overcame him and he was shaken by only an occasional dry sob. By that time Sofia had abandoned all attempt at cooking a dinner.

She said morosely, "While you have your bath I will prepare a tray with cheese, toast and coffee and set it in your room. And see that you eat! There has been enough of trouble for one day."

Laurie took a long while over the bath. The affair had exacted its toll and she was left almost without will and energy. She put on a blue linen housecoat, brushed a vestige of life into her hair and tried a finger of the cheese toast and some coffee. She would have liked to slide into bed but was afraid of falling asleep too soon. It was not yet ten, and she had decided to take a last peep at Richard at about eleven.

So she carried a book into the lounge and sat near a reading lamp, trying to make sense of the printed word. Sofia and Giulo had gone to their room which adjoined the laundry. The native servants had long ago wound their way over the hill to their family hut in the reserve and the house rested in the queer hush which invariably follows upheaval.

Into the quietude came the sound of an approaching car. It stopped, a door slammed and footsteps came up the path; the footsteps of more than one person. Laurie had no time to wonder whether Cedric could be so indiscreet as to show up at this hour before knuckles rapped quietly on the panel of the door. She went into the hall, pulled back the bolt and turned the handle.

That little extra fortitude which ever waits in reserve came to Laurie's aid. She saw who stood there, swung wide the door and stepped back.

"Good evening, senhor."

The woman with Felipe came in first. She wore white chiffon and a flame-colored scarf about her naked shoulders, and her smile was restrained and solicitous. Felipe closed the door and said rapidly:

"Corina, this is Richard's Laurie . . . the Senhora Queira." And without pausing: "Your message has caught up with me a few minutes ago, senhorita. We have been visiting friends on their yacht, Corina and I, and my servants did not know where to find me. What is this which has happened to Richard? Is he sick?"

"Not now, senhor." Possibly Laurie was too drained by the evening's events to be anything but calm. She was able to look at Felipe as steadily as if he were an old acqaintance who had never stirred her pulses, and to return the smile of the senhora. "If you'll come into the lounge I'll explain."

As Corina sank into a chair and Felipe brought forward another, Laurie knew herself at a disadvantage yet was singularly unmoved. This woman was mature and lovely, and perhaps because she had been drinking wine and dancing . . . . and driving with Felipe, her skin had the flush of a tea rose. The flame-colored scarf had fallen, and the beautifully-rounded shoulders gleamed dully in the lamplight; perhaps, at some time during the evening, Felipe had touched his lips to them.

Laurie had no make-up and she knew her hair would be lank from the excessive sweating till she could give it a wash. The housecoat was a good fit but not to be compared with the brocades and soft silks worn by the rich Portuguese. She did not know that her eyes, shadowed grey pools in the pallor of her face, accentuated her look of wistfulness and youth. Nor did she care that even homely linen, when well cut, will reveal the tender curves and hug the waist.

She did her explaining and Felipe listened. He was leaning back on the table, regarding her keenly. When she had finished he bent forward.

"I am sorry, so very sorry that I was out when you sent for me."

"I didn't send for you, senhor. Pedro called at the Palacio without my permission."

The dark eyes narrowed, as if her manner reminded him of their last interview in the Gourros' garden, but he spoke levelly. "I have a right to be told of these things. You must realize that, if we are to do always what is best for the child. It is not that I could do more for him than you could, but I am—what you call proxy, for his parents. It is not necessary for you to hold the whole responsibility."

"I shifted the responsibility to the doctor."

"You did nothing of the sort! It is easy to see that you have exhausted yourself with it, that you punish yourself because you, a stranger to our tropical seas, did not happen to be aware that rarely—so rarely that no one troubles to warn you—we have one dangerous little fish. You wear yourself out, and I repeat, it is not necessary!"

"Felipe, how stern you are." Corina made a laughing interjection. "Laurie has endured enough. You do not mind if I call you Laurie? I like it—because it is different from the Portuguese, and Felipe did not mention your other name. You must be tired."

Her voice, like her looks, was composed and gracious; it had a husky note which in other circumstances and saying other things might be fascinating. Felipe smiled at her, but the smile sharpened when he turned back to Laurie.

"You should be in bed."

"If I had been, there would have been no one to answer you tonight."

"That is not important. I would have gone to the back and roused Sofia." He straightened. "I will come tomorrow. We must go now, Corina."

Corina rose slowly. "In a day or two, when he is quite over this nasty sting, I would like to see the little Richard. I should also like to talk with you, Laurie, because your profession is one which interests me very much. There was a time when I wished to train as a doctor."

Felipe said, "I have told you before that you are too beautiful to be a doctor. Come."

They said good-bye on the step and when they were halfway down the path Laurie closed the door. She remained there with her back against it and her fingers tight on the handle, her ear straining for the starting up of the car. But the car did not start. There were footsteps again, strong, firm ones, alone this time. Once more the quiet tap at the door. Laurie opened it and faced him.

"An apology," said Felipe; half-mockingly. "I had no intention to be sharp with you but for some reason you and I must always cross swords. It is sad, but a fact. You are so proud, so anxious to be independent, and I find I must say the words which will tilt at that pride and independence. You forgive me?"

Her breathing was playing the tricks it had played before when she had been alone with him, and her nerves, which had been dormant, began to quiver. "Of course. It's my fault, really. Some things put me on edge."

"On edge," he said, savoring the syllables. "It is a pictorial expression and very apt. Quite often it has seemed to me that you are on edge, my dear child, and I think what a pity it is that you keep so much of what is in your mind to yourself. Ever since you came to Mondego there has been something which worries you, yes?"

"No!" she contradicted him, swiftly.

He gave the familiar shrug. "But, yes," he said flatly. "One day perhaps you will have to admit it, and if so, you must let me help you. I should like you to come to me if you are in difficulty of any sort—even if it should have a connection with this friend of yours, Maybury." A pause. "I cannot decide whether that young man is a knave or a fool."

"He's not a knave, senhor."

"Ah, but you are no judge. It is said that a degree of blindness accompanies the hypersensitive state of mind and body which is known as being in love."

As usual, he was stimulating her brain to over- activity. Laurie could not help retorting, "You're assuming too much. One does not have to be in love to enjoy a man's company, senhor."

"No," he conceded with charm, "but one has to be a little mentally blind to enjoy the company of a man like Maybury. However, I did not come back to talk about that one. I want to tell you that I admire very much your devotion to Richard, even if you do take your goodness a trifle too far. I will come to see him tomorrow morning at about half past ten, and I hope you will invite me to remain for a cup of chocolate. Not that I drink chocolate, but it is a custom, you understand— the sitting over the cooling liquid while one makes talk with a beautiful woman."

A faint color tinged her cheeks. "Please, senhor. That's too extravagant a compliment, even from you!"

He looked down at her, whimsically. "You do not believe you are beautiful? It is said in your country that beauty is in the eye of the onlooker . . ."

"Beholder," she corrected him, involuntarily.

"Very well, beholder. To me, simplicity has its own deep beauty. You are simple as an English daisy, and as proud and unyielding as the Mondegoan oleander. What can happen to such a combination!"

Weary as she was, she knew again that melting warmth in her very bones. He wasn't only charming and exquisitely courteous. He was . . . rather a dear. A bit of a beast, too, she thought, with a catch in her throat which made her put her hand to it.

He took the hand into his and examined it with concern. "This long scratch at your wrist—is this, also, part of the price of devotion?"

He held the hand too firmly for her to withdraw it. "I caught it on a thorn."

"Better the hand than the heart," he said, "but do not neglect it." Lightly, he bent and put his mouth to the thin trail of inflammation.

Her fingers, when she plunged them into her pocket, contracted nervously. She stood before him, straight and small, eyelids lowered and her chest painfully tight.

"You are very tired," he said gently. "*Boas noites*, little Laurie. Sleep well."

He was gone. The car purred away and after a long silence Laurie pushed home the bolt. Automatically, she looked at her watch. It was only a quarter to eleven. In the last half hour or so she seemed to have lived through a lifetime.

He would take Corina back to Porto Mondego. Did they kiss when they parted? Did he hold her and whisper endearments; did he make her feel that she was above and apart from all the other women in the world? Of course he did. His kindness to Laurie Bell, the small familiarity of using her first name and the gentleness of his tone as he said good night were indicative of an infinitesimal degree of the charm and tenderness he could exert towards the woman he loved.

The demure and aristocratic Corina Queira was indeed blessed above other women. Upon which thought Laurie light-headedly made her way to Richard's bedroom. And as she walked she was pressing the hand his lips had touched to her cheek.

CHAPTER EIGHT

AFTER that, the tempo of Laurie's existence speeded up. Within a day Richard had recovered from his experience on the beach, but the incident drew neighbors to the Casa during most of the following week. They were as sympathetic as if the child had had a serious illness, and brought small gifts for him and bouquets for Laurie.

Almeido Gourros, his oiled hair brushed back in deep, luxuriant waves and a camellia in the lapel of his beige linen jacket, brought a pot plant which he told her was basil that his mother had reared from a cutting he himself had carried back from Lisbon a few months ago.

"Watch the buds closely," he begged her. "In this climate the plant often wilts before the bud can open, but if they do open, they will have a message for you."

Laurie had no idea what he meant, but being a lover of herbs and having an affection for all tiny struggling things, she took the pot of basil to her heart and gave it the cofee-cup full of water each day that he prescribed.

She liked Almeido Gourros. Indeed, she liked all the young Portuguese. Isabel was always planning something; a ride to some other spot on the coast, a day at the races in Porto, an evening's fishing in an outrigger, or a midnight party round a camp fire. Invariably, because he was new and therefore interesting, she contrived an invitation for Cedric, and whenever he could extricate himself from potential customers he accepted. He was always irritated by Laurie's absence from the merry-making.

Here in Mondego his natural gaiety seemed to have deserted him. He knew that Laurie had gained prestige among the people of Villa Barreiro because the Marquez had become a frequent caller at the Casa, and he also knew that he himself had no aura of romance—he was a change, that was all. Sometimes he thought that even Isabel, who flashed a wicked eye and tossed a pretty curl, was laughing at him. Which was a new and unpalatable experience, for he had not yet learned that she was already betrothed to a man in Portugal.

But it was Laurie who really hurt. He could tell she had made up her mind that there was little to be gained from renewing their friendship. His proposal had meant nothing at all, and her chief concern seemed to be to know the date when he would be leaving; which was a frightful knock to his self-esteem. She had said they would have fun together, and then dropped out of the running. She would even drive into Porto Mondego to see him for half an hour. Yet she was relying on him to keep secret the fact that she was Laurie Fielding, sister to Senhora Alvares.

She puzzled him, and he didn't care to be puzzled by someone whom he had hitherto considered as transparent and refreshing as spring water. Sometimes he felt he ought to teach Laurie a lesson, but so far he had been deterred by pleasant memories of long summer days in her company—mild days, not the blistering, sweaty kind that followed each other with devitalising regularity here in Mondego. How he loathed this climate!

He liked temperateness in all things. That was why he desired Laurie; because hers would be a moderate, thoughtful kind of passion, not the consuming thing which seemed to flash like darts of lightning between these Portuguese. Though he was less sure about her than previously.

When he called at the Casa for a few minutes one morning before attending one of Isabel's functions, Laurie had looked odd: sort of tense, yet unable to hide an inward glow. Cedric pondered, but for the present could reach no conclusion. This island could do anything to anyone. But Laurie?

She would have been surprised and scared had she known his thoughts. She had done that fatal thing: neglected to take seriously a proposal from a man who had all the stubborn pride of the weak. As it happened, she had never thought him really weak; her adjectives for Cedric had been kinder. Easy-going, debonair, popular. Not a man to whom one would turn in trouble, perhaps, but likeable, none the less. She would never have believed that such a character could have a mild streak of viciousness. It took a letter from Stella to disclose that fact.

Stella wrote that she and Eduardo were having a simply marvellous time. "It is such a relief to know that Richard is in your care, and it has made all the difference to this tour. We're doing all the things we haven't been able to do before. By the time you receive this letter our absence from Mondego will have reached the halfway line. . ."

Laurie broke off there. Good heavens, yes! Stella had been gone a month. Just one month to go, which Laurie desperately hoped would not pass as swiftly as the first. She would have liked to stay on at the Casa Margarita for much longer, and not only for Richard's sake.

About life at the moment there was a dangerous sweetness which she could not fully analyze. It had to do with the way these people of Villa Barreiro accepted her and with Richard's increasing good health, with the fact of her being mistress of the house, and with the visits of Felipe every two or three days—mostly it had to do with the visits of Felipe. That was why the sweetness held danger. But not such a lot of danger, Laurie told herself firmly, because she was wide awake to all the implications of allowing her emotions to be swayed by the Marquez. No girl in her senses would do that.

Laurie had yet to learn that the senses are sometimes traitors.

It was during her second reading of Stella's letter that she remembered Cedric. He must have been here nearly a month—a month, and he was as undecided about his departure as when he first came! She had let the time slip by, trusting that the necessity for dispossessing of his pictures would curtail his stay. In any case, it had never occurred to her for a second that he would hang on so long. What was he thinking of!

Laurie laid aside Stella's letter and looked at her watch. Nine-thirty. Time to get into Porto Mondego and back again before the midday heat. She must definitely go. From the french door she called Richard.

"We're going for a drive, darling. Let me make you tidy."

While he submitted to having his hands washed, Richard recited, "There was an old woman who lived in a shoe." He now soaked up rhymes with astonishing ease and seldom got a word wrong when he repeated them. While Laurie went off to collect her purse, he finished one rhyme and started another in his high-pitched, chanting voice.

"Bow, wow, wow," she heard him say, "Whose dog art thou?"

He was answered in the deep, vital tones which invariably made Laurie's heart miss a beat. "I am the dog of Rodrigo Gomez!"

A shriek. "Tio Felipe! You are little Tom Tucker's dog."

"Indeed I am not. I would not be the dog of a boy with such a name. I am the dog of Rodrigo Gomez—no less! Where is Laurie?"

She knew that he only spoke of her thus, with conspiratorial friendliness, when addressing the child, but the knowledge could not stop the tiny electric shock of pleasure in the way he said her name. She came to the lounge door, met his eyes across the room.

"Good morning, senhor. You're early."

"And you, my dear Miss Bell, are fresher than the morning sunshine. I am free till lunch time, and propose to take you back to the Palacio for talks with the fishes and flowers. Perhaps I will also show you some of my little collections. That will suit you?"

The realized urgency of the visit to Porto Mondego showed in her hesitation. She had waited so long that a further half-day could matter little, yet she was afraid that if she did not see Cedric this morning he might be impossible to contact later, which would mean a day wasted. And the days were suddenly very valuable.

"You had some other plan?" asked Felipe.

"I was just getting ready to go into Porto Mondego."

"For shopping?"

"No. Merely a short visit on business."

"Then I will drive you there, and straight back to the Palacio."

She had moved towards the french door, and looked up at him smiling. "I can't trouble you to do that, senhor. I'll postpone my business till tomorrow."

"But, no. We will fit it in. If we can return to the Palacio by eleven there will still be two hours before my luncheon appointment, and one can do much in two hours. Come, my big Ricardo, we will march to the auto!"

But just inside the french door, near to Laurie, he stopped, for his glance was caught by the pot plant which stood behind the jar of flowers on a small table. He bent and picked it up from the brass plate on which it rested, sniffed at the small green leaves and gave Laurie a mocking smile.

"So you have a Portuguese suitor. Did this young man explain the custom?"

"He only said that when the flowers opened they would have a message for me."

"A message of love," Felipe elucidated. "It is merely a preliminary, you understand? In Portugal a young man gives the pot of basil to the girl who attracts him. He adjures her to tend it well in order that it may flourish and when it flowers he declares his love. He has planted the seed but it cannot mature unless it is cared for by the woman. Which, you will agree, is true of love. This one," with a smile, "must be a hot-headed young man, for I see you take much trouble to keep the plant cool and green."

She laughed a little. "I took so much care because it looked rather weedy. I may bother less now that I know the meaning of the custom."

Felipe was still smiling down at her with faint mockery. "If you wish not to hurt his feelings there is a way out. Find a spot in the garden which the sun does not reach, and transplant the basil. You will thus show the young Almeido that you value his affection, but cannot accord to him more favor than you do to the other friends—other flowers. He will comprehend."

"How did you know Almeido gave it to me?"

"One detects and draws conclusions. He has good English—the rest have not. He has polish, temerity and good taste. There is not one among the others who would dare to think of you in such terms," a pause, "and you—does it intrigue you to be the chosen of a Portuguese?"

"It's flattering," she said, "but I'm afaraid I could never love Almeido."

"I thought so." He passed into the verandah, adding nonchalantly, "I think you would be scared of love as the Portuguese make it."

It was like him to make a challenging statement and give her no time to parry it. Not that she would have known what to say, she admitted, as she went down the path at his side and got into his car. But he needn't have cut the talk short by striding out like that.

Since Richard's adventure with the stingray Felipe had been kind and comradely and ever-available. They had discussed many things and he had rallied her in the courteous, teasing manner which was peculiar to Felipe, compelled her to put some of her naive conclusions about Mondego into words. Sometimes, when his satire lost its smiling quality, she was sorry he had tempted her to air her opinions. When he disagreed he could be forceful, even dictatorial.

Today, however, Laurie could not rise to him. She looked out at the thorn and wild nut trees, at the tiny iron houses near which dozens of Indian children played, at the tangles of scarlet poinsetta, the trails of pink-flowering liana which smothered cycads and gnarled old rubber trees, and she wondered how she could posibly concoct some sort of business in Mondego which would stir no suspicions in Felipe.

It would be horribly difficult to lie to him. But why should she want to deceive him? She had every right to see Cedric and what she had to say to him would not take long. Yes, it was really best to behave openly as far as possible. Felipe could not disapprove of a brief, business-like encounter at this hour. Yet when he asked where he should stop for her, her reply began with a stammer.

"The . . . the Hotel Carnac, please."

The atmosphere within the car changed infinitesimally. Felipe said politely, with frank perceptiveness, "The hotel? You wish then to see Maybury?"

"Yes, senhor." She should have been airy and demanded, "You have no objection?" But the change in atmosphere was becoming more pronounced every second and she identified it as emanating from a distinct chill, which would not be lessened by truculence. So she added, "I told you it could have waited till tomorrow. I'll be quick."

Nothing more was said just then. The car ran in from the coast road on to the Esplanada and in no time at all had pulled up in the hotel courtyard. With the swift, almost animal grace which characterized all his movements, he was out on the driveway and round the car to open her door.

"We will go into the lounge," he said, "and have a small drink. Perhaps this countryman of yours will join us. There are things I should like to ask him."

Sincerely, Laurie hoped to avoid a meeting between Felipe and Cedric. Yet to go with Cedric to one of the more private rooms, even for a few minutes, was bound to be damaging. She was begining to wish that Felipe had stayed at the Palacio this morning. He complicated everything.

"Will you excuse me, senhor?"

"Certainly," he answered, with the utmost politeness.

She left his side and went to the reception desk. The clerk was smiling as he would have smiled at any woman who might accompany the Marquez; a nasty, fawning smile Laurie thought it, in her vexation.

"What can I do for you, senhora?"

"Can you tell me if Mr. Maybury is in his room?"

"I regret, senhora—the Senhor Inglez is out; I do not know where, but he will surely return for lunch. Would the senhora care to leave a message?"

Suggestively, he pushed a writing block towards her. Unready with any idea of what to write, she accepted the proffered pen and bit on her lip. Felipe was eight or nine feet away, unconcernedly flipping the pages of a brochure he had taken from a table; yet he seemed near and forbidding. In something of a maze, Laurie wrote: "I must see you soon, Cedric. Will you come to the Casa during siesta time today or tomorrow—not later than tomorrow, please!"

She slipped the note into an envelope, sealed it and addressed it. When the clerk had assured her that Mr. Maybury would receive the letter as he came in, she turned to Felipe with some relief.

"Cedric is out, I'm told, so my business with him will have to wait."

"He will, however," said Felipe with a sharp and not-too-pleasant smile, "have a message from you to warm his heart in the meantime. Let us have this drink we promised ourselves, and go."

"Can't we go at once and have the drink at the Palacio? Unless, senhor," she said deliberately, her pulses drumming, "you have changed your mind and would prefer to take us back to the Casa."

The thinning of his lips was vividly reminiscent of a scene she had tried, during the last week or two, to forget; the two of them under an archway of bougainvillea, his fingers digging cruelly into her arm.

"No, Miss Bell," he replied, flint in his tone. "I have not changed my mind—about anything. Nor do I break promises; Richard shall see his fish, and for his sake you must tolerate them."

Laurie did not go inside the Palacio that morning, though sitting on the terrace with a tall lime and soda she knew the previous sensation of delicious awe engendered by the age and distinctiveness of the architecture, and the great sweep of gardens and lawns beyond the balustrade. Felipe, however, seemed disinclined to linger in conversation, though it was no effort for him to be kind to Richard.

He led them to where the tinkling fountains rose like slender plumes of tropic grass in the still air and spilled their effervescence in rainbow showers; he stopped at the pools in which brilliant fish darted and spun and told them the names and origins of the exotic species.

"This little fellow of scarlet and blue-green with the transparent fins is the neon tetra—a lovely example, do you not agree? He came from the Pacific. Those pinkish-white things which move as if they feel the heat of the sun are cave fish—very rare, but not very attractive. And here we have the veil-tail betta. What coloring, and each one different! Red, blue, green and the pretty shade of lavender. You have heard of the Siamese fighting fish, Miss Bell? Well, here it is, fierce and beautiful."

"Did you yourself collect the fish, senhor?"

"I have added a few specimens, but the collection was started by my mother when she came here as a bride." It was said offhandedly, as though to discourage further questions, but after a moment he tacked on, "She studied the subject closely and had the pools sanded and set with suitable aquatic plants before putting in the fish. We have altogether one hundred and fifty species—about ten times as many fish altogether, and none to my knowledge has ever died except of old age."

When it was time for Richard to go, Felipe put him into the car but instructed a chauffeur to drive. He stood beside the car, dark, alert, magnetic, but still coldly aloof, and looked down at Laurie.

"I trust you have had an instructive morning, Miss Bell? More instructive than pleasing, I think you will say. I am afraid one cannot help that." A shrug. "I had been going to make an arrangement for Richard to sleep here one night, so that you could dine with some friends and myself, but we will leave it for a while."

Then why mention it, fumed Laurie to herself; she felt she could stand no more of him in this mood. She turned to get in beside Richard, but those long, sensitive fingers were laid lightly upon her arm.

"One last word," he said, in a tone both rapid and low and calculated to preclude the possibility of the chauffeur catching a word or two of unfamiliar English. "I know about men and you know very little; you will admit that. You are very foolish to remain friendly with this Maybury. If you have any influence with him use it for your own good and send him away."

Laurie stared at him, saw the glinting eyes, the mouth still compressed. Panic fluttered in her veins. What did he suspect? Could it possibly be that he realized Cedric had a hold over her? Surely not. He had been given no cause for suspicion. Yet why else should he speak to her like this?

She trembled under his touch and instantly he said quietly, "You are not to be anxious, my dear Laurie. I have purposely refrained from speaking to this man because I respect your friendship for him—as I would respect your friendship for anybody—but I will be happy to deal with him for you. I assure you," with crispness, "that I can make him leave Mondego by the next boat."

"No!" She had answered precipitately, and now had to pause to gather her wits and mute her tones. "I can handle it. I prefer to."

"You need do nothing—merely leave it to me."

Felipe of the high hand, ordering the art dealer to be gone. And how would Cedric react to that? She shook her head quickly. "Thank you for offering, but I'll do it myself."

He didn't like her decision; she could see that. But she kept her head up and her chin firm, and at last he responded, "Very well. He is your friend and you have the right. But will you come to me if it is at all difficult?"

"Yes," she promised recklessly. "I will."

She was inside the car and it moved away. She saw his head bent in farewell, his upraised hand and the tight, suave smile which invariably accomapnied his "*Adieus!*"

CHAPTER NINE

ALL THROUGH lunch she willed Cedric to come today. Unless he was having an all-day session with one of his prospects she felt sure he would turn up, and then her problem would be how to disguise from him the fact that his presence in Mondego menaced both her peace of mind and her friendship with Felipe.

This morning, after reading Stella's letter, it had all looked much simpler; she had thought she would not even have to allude to those cheques which meant so much to her father and which Stella had threatened to withhold; that kind of thing was too private to be told to Cedric, who knew Henry Fielding. She had intended to appeal to Cedric's essential decency, to point out that he was much more likely to sell his pictures in Paris or Brussels and that the sooner he got to one or the other the happier for all concerned. The idea of a talk with him had been distasteful but not really frightening.

Since the brief discussion with Felipe, however, the whole matter had a sinister cast. It appeared fantastic to connect Cedric, who normally drifted gaily through life without ill-will to anyone and was thoroughly well-liked, with anything sinister, but she could not dispel the feeling. It was completely crazy, and the sooner he could be persuaded to leave the island the safer for her own sanity; it was certainly precariously balanced at the moment. She was beginning to doubt whether she could stand much more uncertainty and agitation.

Having missed his morning sleep, Richard dozed within a few minutes of climbing into his cot. Laurie had a wash and changed into a white linen frock, and then she went into the cool, dim lounge, to read, and hope.

It was twenty minutes to three when the taxi stopped outside, with much more noise than Laurie deemed necessary, and Cedric, in the quick, quiet fashion which she had so often marvelled at in so rugged-looking a man, made his way up the path and into the porch.

He did not have to knock or ring a bell. Laurie was there, smiling a little nervously and raising a finger to her lips to enjoin silence till he should be inside, with the door closed.

"Everbody's asleep," she explained, "and I want to get our talk over before they awaken. I'm so glad you could come today, Cedric."

He looked at her, his blue glance unusually shrewd, yet puzzled. Had she been less disturbed she would have interpreted that glance of Cedric's and perhaps have contrived a greater subtelty. But it did not occur to her to measure her adversary; Cedric was her friend.

"Of course I came," he said. "You know that I've only been waiting for an invitation."

She did look his way then, but, without discernment, "We should have got together before this," she said. "Have a cigarette?"

"One on the house? Thanks." He selected a cigarette from the black box she offered, twisted it meditatively between his fingers; his mouth pulled into a crooked smile. "We're matey, aren't we? It's so sudden that I'm dazed with the wonder of it."

Reining her nerves, she willed herself to hold her own cigarette steadily to his match and to inhale slowly before answering: "I've never before thought of asking you to come at siesta time. It's peaceful, isn't it?"

"Very peaceful." He eyed her almost sardonically through the smoke. "What do I do now? Relax in a chair, become bemused by my good fortune and tranquility, and agree to whatever you suggest?"

She had become taut inside, taut and fearful. This was far trickier than anything she had anticipated. Cedric was ruffled and he was not blind; he could see that, maybe unconsciously, she was setting the scene for the real purpose of this interview; somehow she couldn't avoid giving that impression. Her smile was not successful.

"You think," she said, "that I'm going to ask you to do something for me—something distasteful. But I'm not, Cedric. You're behaving oddly—differently from what I expected. Before I go any further I should like your assurance that we're still friends."

"That assurance should come from you, not from me. I've told you before that I'm willing to marry you as soon as I can afford it. I'll tell you again, if you like."

"We're not in love; you know that. You can't make a go of marriage without love. But if you do care for me a little it makes what I have to say a bit easier. Cedric," she faltered a fraction but tried valiantly to gloss it, "I'm horribly afraid that if you stay much longer in Mondego I shall be in a serious fix. You see . . ."

"The 'Miss Bell' affair?" he cut in. The mouth she had always thought slack but by no means ugly, drew in more firmly and showed obstinate dents at the corners. "I've been accommodating, haven't I? Accepted the detail or two you confessed and asked no questions; the complete diplomat. I took it to be a harmless arrangement between you and your sister, but it appears to have some importance."

"Not to anyone else!" she exclaimed. "We're hurting no one, but it would hurt us both if it ever became known that we're sisters."

"So you want me to get out in case Senhora Alvares suspects that I'm aware of her little secret." He paused. "As a matter of fact, she's the very reason I'm hanging on. These pieces I'm managing to sell won't even pay my hotel bill, but they're something to do while I wait for the arrival of the senhora. I've discovered an item you didn't tell me, Laurie. Your sister isn't ordinarily rich—she's a fabulously wealthy woman, and it's on the cards that she may buy the Tintoretto."

Laurie went white. She shook away ash and drew on the cigarette, her brain feverishly grappling with this new peril. She felt as if the world were slipping away from under her feet. To gain time she said, "I don't understand you at all. You're different—hard and unsympathetic."

"No," he said. "I'm like you—a shade desperate. When I came to Mondego I was full of eagerness and fire. I was terribly keen to see you and was pretty certain that you'd be joyful at the sight of me, too. Also, I had no doubts about the picture; the Marquez was my man. Well, I got a shock on both counts, and I haven't recovered from either of them yet. You haven't treated me fairly, Laurie."

Unhappily, she shook her head. "Would it have been fair to lead you on? I don't think so, and in your heart you don't think so, either. I couldn't have seen much of you, anyway. Richard keeps me tied here most of the time."

"But you did squeeze in a call at my hotel this morning," he reminded her with irony. "It appears that you do have time for your own ends. I'm sorry to speak to you like this, Laurie, but if you've ever been hurt by someone from whom you least expected it, you know how I feel now."

"I'm sorry, Cedric. It wouldn't have worked."

He pressed on. "You were glad when the noble Marquez put a stop to my coming here, weren't you? You knew I loathed the climate of the island and took it for granted that once he'd turned down the picture I'd clear out and try elsewhere. You banked on that, didn't you? But I didn't go, because I hadn't so likely a client on my list. And now I've left it too late."

"Too late?" she echoed thinly. This session with Cedric was growing beyond reality. She had imagined herself doing most of the talking, and Cedric being facetious and slightly hopeless in his outlook but never an enemy. Now, she was learning his thoughts, and they made her wish she had come to know them earlier, before the bitterness had crept in. She could have managed him easily then.

His shoulders lifted and he spoke with his old, smiling casualness. "Yes, too late, my pet. Too late to go back without having sold the thing. You know the exorbitant charges at the Carnac, and there's no other hotel. I've already overdrawn my expense account by a good many pounds, but that will be overlooked if I take back the cheque for the Tintoretto. Without that cheque I'm in a large-sized financial jam and possibly out of a job."

Laurie could no longer sit still. She went to the french door and looked out, saw the foolish pot of basil behind the flower-jar and wondered if such situations as this ever shadowed the lives of people like Almeido and Isabel. She turned back.

"Stella has no interests in the arts. I don't think for a moment that she'd buy your picture."

"She might," he said," to get rid of me."

The early afternoon heat swept into the room in a gust. It brought the faint but heavy scent of tropical shrubs, the smell of weed washed high by the tide and the lazy trilling of a bird.

Clearly she saw what would happen if Cedric were here when Stella returned. Stella might, as he said, buy the picture to get rid of him, but she would undoubtedly suspect Laurie and was capable of doing her worst in well-bred revenge. Laurie would have to go, and those cheques to York would cease. Stella had known what she was about when she had voiced that threat!

"Don't look like that. I'm not trying to frighten you, Laurie," he said, more softness in his tone. "I don't *have* to stay till your sister returns. There's another way, but you'll have to help."

"Anything!" she told him quickly.

"Well, we come back to the Marquez and his lucre. Somehow, you must persuade him to buy the Tintoretto."

"I?" She stiffened and spoke incredulously. "How in the world do you suppose I can influence his decisions? You must be mad."

"You're a woman—a damned pretty one—and he's a friend of yours."

"He's Richard's godfather; and I happen to be Richard's nurse!"

"Is that all?" He was maliciously bland, as if he knew himself in control. "I heard that he brought you to the hotel this morning and it was thought that you were going back to the Palacio with him."

"All that was purely accidental, because he happened to call when I was ready to leave. He does his duty by Richard, no more. I can't possibly approach him for you."

"That's too bad, because I'm quite sure that if he had another good look at the thing he'd buy it. He knows you and I have been acquainted for a number of years and he's unlikely to think it strange it you ask him to give the picture another once-over. It's the sort of thing any woman might do for a friend."

"He'd only turn it down again. He's told me himself that it's not a good Tintoretto.'

"Then try to prove him wrong, my sweet," he said a little sharply. "You underrate yourself. You're English, fair of skin and charmingly different from the dark and sparkling Portuguese, whom I daresay he knows far too well. Even the lovely Corina can't boast of being so very different from her countrywomen. And you can bet that a connoisseur like Felipe is entirely conscious of every grace that you have which the others haven't; that kind of knowledge is in his very bones. *You* can sell him that picture, and if you're dying for my departure you'll go right ahead and do it. Think around a bit and you'll find there's nothing else for it."

And that, it seemed, was the extent of what he had to say. When she protested he could only repeat it in other words. Ten minutes later, before Sofia or Richard had roused, Cedric went his way, and Laurie was left leaning nervelessly against the verandah wall and slowly realizing that there was, indeed, nothing for it but to approach Felipe on Cedric's behalf. But how to attack so delicate a task was, at this moment, quite beyond her comprehension.

For the next couple of days Mondego was battered by a series of storms. As is common in the islands east of Africa, winds of cyclonic intensity accompanied the rain, and Laurie experienced her first complete shut-in.

To Sofia this was a normal, if infrequent, occurrence. She and Giulio, with the help of a native servant, secured the shutters over the windows and glass doors. The crack under every door which led outside was sealed with a *salchicha*, a long thin "sausage" made from a black stocking stuffed with rags, and all locks and catches were examined for the possible rusty one which might give way and precipitate a catastrophe.

The electricity failed—it always did at such times, said Sofia—and paraffin lamps had to be kept burning all day. It was an eerie business, walking about by lamplight in the shuttered house while rain beat about it like a thousand devils and the wind roared louder than the thunder. Sunny, langorous Mondego was turning with a vengeance upon those who took her even temper for granted.

Sofia told tales of shipwreck in the tumultuous seas, of Indians washed down from their flimsy homes, of rivers creating broad lakes in the plantations and of monkeys clawing at house shutters for the shelter which could not be given them.

"Even," Sofia stated with pride, "we have found crocodile from the Guarez River flung into the sea and up on to our beach. You will be astonished at the things which will be found on the sand after this. It is said that these storms also have effect on the island people. Afterwards there are troubles in families, broken engagements and jealousy." A deep, Latin shrug. "But what would you? The wind touches the nerves of the young and restless with red hot wires; the imprisonment is only tolerable to the old like Giulio and me."

In her present condition of unrest and apprehension, the respite was not intolearble to Laurie, either. Till the stormy spell was over everything had to stand still, and her only regret was that time also could not be made to halt. She knew that as soon as the weather became fair enough to permit the fastening back of the shutters she would have to act for Cedric, and the knowledge lay like lead in her mind and heart. At present she could only contain it, not think about it.

When she rested she thought of all the other houses in Villa Barreiro, their occupants incarcerated as she was, their gardens wind-torn and channelled with water. The Palacio, of course, owned a reserve lighting plant, and according to Giulio some of the dozens of back windows had been fitted with transparent plastic shutters, so that Felipe could, if he wished, watch the chaos in his gardens.

She dragged her thoughts from Felipe and sent them to Porto Mondego, where a ship or two might be anchored and little craft wrenched from their frail moorings and broken on the rocks. The shops and hotel would be closed right up, and only the breakers, hurling stones on the wind, would have possession of the waterfront.

"What about those lovely flowering trees along the esplanade at Porto?" she asked Sofia. "Will they be up-rooted?"

"Many of them, yes. But the new ones grow swiftly. There is always a reserve in the municipal gardens—big plants in great fibre pots made from the coconut palm which can be set straight into the soil. Those pots go to bits, you understand, and help to fertilize the plants."

"Every one seems to be prepared for this."

"It is to be prepared," answered Sofia with philosophical pessimism, and a wave of a bony brown hand to embrace shutters, paraffin lamps and *salchicas* along the bottoms of the doors, "or almost certain death. No one could live for long in the streets. Do not worry, *minha menina.* It will not last longer than two days."

During the first day, while the sensation of being sealed off from the world was suffocatingly new, Laurie was unable to settle. She helped Richard to build houses with his bricks, to colour-in pictures and to set up a collapsible farmhouse which was among his toys; and every hour or so she suggested, in order to make up for the lack of exercise, that he imitate the soldiers who occasionally drilled on the wide stone waterfront above the harbour at Villa Barreiro. As children will, Richard enjoyed the novelty of being imprisoned.

On the second day, however, Laurie was calmer. In spite of Sofia's assurance to the contrary, it seemed as if the torrential rain and the driving wind would never cease; as if she were enclosed in the Casa Margarita for ever. Which meant, of course, that she need trouble about nothing beyond these walls. And what a blessing that was!

To please Sofia and for something to do, she took part in some Portuguese cooking. Chickens braised with ham, pork and many vegetables and deliciously seasoned with sweet pepper and shreds of saffron; omelette packed with mushrooms and chopped bacon and served in a nest of mashed, buttered potatoes; fish rolls baked with slices of pineapple and smothered in cheese sauce; pastry cases piled high with a mixture of sardine, finely chopped beetroot and hard boiled egg covered with a seasoned dressing.

The coolest cupboard in the pantry filled with nutty biscuits, honey cakes and fruit tartlets, all of which Giulio, who sat near the paraffin cooker which had to be used because there was no dry fuel for the wood stove, sampled straight from the oven.

It was towards evening that the gale dropped. Laurie sat in the lounge mending a tear in one of Richard's shirts when suddenly she became conscious of a lessening of noise which amounted to a comparative stillness. Her head rose as she listened, and then, filled with an uneasy excitement, she jumped up and was about to go to the kitchen when Sofia appeared at the doorway.

"It is finished." The lined face was unsmiling, the tone unemotional. "Soon you will hear the church bells, unless they have been damaged, but no one will go out before daylight tomorrow. You hear? There is not even any rain."

No, no rain, and only enough wind to cause a rustling in the trees and a whispering in the grass. The tension within the house did not ease, it snapped. Giulio slapped his knee and gave hearty laughs, Richard shouted and stamped though he knew not why, Sofia whipped up the sodden, mud-caked *salchicas* and opened the ventilators, and Laurie stitched frenziedly to keep time with her chaotic thoughts.

It was Thursday, and she had promised Cedric she would get in touch with him during the week-end. She had one day, perhaps two. She shrank from seeking an interview with Felipe and had no illusions about the outcome, but it had to be done. Whatever the cost to herself, Cedric must go from Mondego before Stella's return.

She finished the sewing and stood on tiptoe to peer through the slats of a ventilator at a sky of warm amber shot with the purple of dusk. A sky so beneficient that it was difficult to revive memories of the cyclone which had petered out such a short while ago. But she could not dispel the feeling of baffled excitement. It was as though she had been suspended, sleeping, in space, and allowed to drop back into normal living without warning.

She must get Richard's supper, set about the mundane details which would soon disperse this stupidness. Every one must be feeling an exaltation of relief, she told herself; it was the aftermath of thunderous wind and hammering rain, the being shut in with poor lights. So childish to allow one's emotions to be worked up and down by the weather.

But the loud tattoo on the front door alarmed her into immobility. Sofia shuffled through to the hall and heaved back the bolt.

"Senhor Marquez!" Laurie heard her exclaim, and proceed in excitable Portuguese: "We are honoured that the senhor should come as soon as the storm is ended. No one but the gracious senhor would dare to venture in the half-light, with trees and roofs across the roads."

Felipe answered her kindly, and Laurie, a hand hard to her side to quell a bounding, physical pain, crossed the room and went into the hall. Felipe looked up from addressing Sophia.

"I hear you are all well here, senhorita. No mishaps... no bad moods?"

"We've come through well, senhor, thank you. It's exceedingly kind of you to call."

Sofia curtsied and withdrew. Felipe came nearer and said in considerate tones, "You were frightened? I am not surprised. The noise is tremendous in a small house and there is always the danger of a collapsing wall. But you were safe here. I thought about you, and was happy to know you were here, and not at the hotel."

His concern was for Richard, Laurie sternly assured herself. He had thought about Laurie as an adjunct to Richard. Before she could frame some kind of reply the bells pealed, victoriously thin and clear in the washed air. Grey eyes met the dark ones in a warm, shared appreciation.

"Bells in thanksgiving are always a good sound," said Felipe. "I must go into the town. There may be some who need help and the thing must be organized."

"Senhor," urgency brought her fingers to his cuff; "when shall we see you again?"

Was it surprise or an echo of his earlier concern that seemed to glitter in his glance? His voice was thoughtful and reserved. "You are bored with two days' inactivity, but that will soon pass now and the skies are clearing. Be thankful that you did not have to face disaster, as others have. My place now is with them."

She was stung to retort: "I know that. If it were possible I'd wade in myself. I wasn't trying to keep you here." The hurt of his misunderstanding rose to her throat. "I apologize for detaining you, senhor."

He laughted briefly. "Ah, again the pride. I think I see. You have said to yourself. 'I will demand of Felipe a small favor—only a small one because I am too proud to accept from him anything which really matters.' Am I right?"

"No, you're quite wrong," she said sharply. "At a time like this I wouldn't want to consult you about anything unimportant."

His manner changed with disconcerting speed, and peremptorily he urged, "Tell me of this now. You know that I am at your command."

This beastly Portuguese chivalry, she thought, suppressing a hysterical laugh. At her command, indeed! One might as well order about a bar of tempered steel.

"It will take too long, and your people's plight may be bad. May I see you tomorrow?"

He meditated for a moment. "Keep Sofia in the house," he said without expression. "I will come back."

She was startled. "Tonight?"

"Yes, tonight. I could, of course, assure you now that I will handle this matter, whatever it is, which disturbs you, but you would still lie pondering it into the night. It is much wiser to attack it at once."

She turned slightly from the aloof smile which moved his lips. "When you've heard, you may not wish to help me."

"That is true," he agreed smoothly. "But I shall help you nevertheless. Till later, my dear Laurie."

She glimpsed the darkening garden as the door opened, saw with extraordinary clarity an uprooted bush caught in the low branches of another. Then he was gone.

CHAPTER TEN

Before she had even closed the door it came to her, rather sickeningly, that Felipe had avoided mentioning Cedric Maybury. But perhaps he had not thought of Cedric, and she was imagining complications where none as yet existed.

She had to get an impersonal slant on this, give Felipe no openings for ridicule or mockery. She must put it to him that he might have been a little unjust to Cedric and it was only fair to give him another chance to display his wares. Felipe unjust? He might be, if something angered him, but even in anger she didn't think he would be unjust to "my dear Laurie."

She knew enough of Portuguese idiom not to be deceived by the ironical suggestion of affection in that term. He called her Laurie because Richard did, and his hint that she thought of him as Felipe had probably been hasty and unintentional.

She was afraid of the sweetness of intimacy, afraid of what it was doing to her inmost being. Yet when she had put Richard to bed that evening and was able to give time to her toilet, she was lapped in the pleasure it gave her to dress in plain green silk and make the brown-gold hair smooth and shining for Felipe. Gently, she touched up her lips with light red and used a brush to her eyelashes. She wished she might be sure that he would notice, and approve.

"The Senhor Marquez is coming again this evening," she had casually told Sofia. "Will you and Giulio stay in the house after dinner?"

A nod. "I am glad he troubles so much with us. He has a great love for the child."

Think what you like, sang Laurie's heart, but tonight . . . tonight Felipe comes only to see me! It would have been a thought to cause delirium had she not been burdened with the weight of Cedric. And even so, there was no denying the joy of anticipation.

He came at about a quarter to nine, and even before he had seen her seated she felt that an atmosphere of drama had entered the room with him. He chose to smoke one of his own rich cigarettes, and as he relaxed into his chair the peculiar gold light showed small lines at the corners of his eyes. She experienced the queer thrust of worry which is natural to a woman when she senses an unwonted weariness in the man she loves.

"Was it dreadful down there in the town?" she asked quietly.

"No worse than after the storm of a year ago. A few small houses lost their roofs, but they will be repaired at once. The streets are choked with driftwood and weed, shutters have disappeared and windows are broken, but there were few casualties and no deaths. Material damage is soon put right. We have been lucky."

"Will there be any way in which I can help tomorrow?" she queried.

"I am providing food for those who are unable to cook. You, also, might give something of that kind; there cannot be too much."

"Gladly." She smiled, willing the tautness from the room. "Sofia and I passed the time by doing a lot of baking today. I'd decided, if our native servants turn up tomorrow, to send one of them back to the reserve with as much food as we can spare."

A faint warmth came into his expression. "That is kind—a really kind intention, and I will not alter it. In fact, we will make something of this. I will send a jeep to call at all the larger houses for a donation of cooked food to be distributed out there in the reserve. Our European dishes do not fill the African, but they will certainly cheer him!"

Laurie bean to feel better; though she could not erase the mortifying conviction that Felipe had come here more from a sense of duty than from inclination; she felt that he didn't want to be here at all. Before something in him she was humble but she knew it unwise to show humility to such a man—nearly as unwise as it was to defy him.

So she remarked conversationally, "This climate of yours is disconcerting, isn't it? A little like the Portuguese themselves."

"You find us disconcerting?" The mockery was back in his tones, making him normal and charming. "You mean that we are mostly gay, but occasionally unexpectedly fierce and cruel, yes?"

"Not all of you."

His eyes glinted. "Perhaps I alone am the object of your disapproval. You think that friendship should be more accommodating, less . . . how shall I say, inquisitive? It annoys you that I probe and give advice which I expect to be followed."

Her instinct was one of self-preservation. She had known he was impossible to deceive, but his quick driving at the point, the shrewd half-smile as if he were aware just what she was about to ask, called up her defences. She was not ready yet.

"One makes a harmless observation and you take possession of it and turn it into a rapier," she said.

Further to ensure that he did not at once pursue the topic, she got up, went to the window and made a complication of setting it a notch wider. She remained there, looking out at the night, and when Felipe came beside her she said softly:

"You must admit this climate is odd. So savage a few hours ago, and now as sleek as silk."

"The air is always like this after such a gale—a draught of chilled wine in a crystal cup. It reminds me of the autumn nights in Portugal. After the grapes have been trodden and everywhere is the smell of fermenting wine, the people dance and sing; it is the custom. At the end of the wine-making there is a *festa,* and in some parts it is known as the *festa* of the merry bachelors, because many bethrothals are made at that time, and afterwards, it is presumed, the bachelors are no longer gay!"

She smiled into the darkness. "I've heard about this wine-making which seems to be a stimulant to lovers. To me, they don't seem to need much stimulation."

Satire clipped his tones. "A quaint people, these Portuguese. At one time carefree and elusive, at another violent and ruthless, and still again they linger under a moon such as this and the man tells the woman she has a mouth as red as a rose and sweet as grapes, and skin smooth and scented as magnolia petals. Such extravagance of phrase would fill you—an English miss—with awkwardness. Sometimes I wonder how it is that you English arrive at marriage!"

"Yet we do. It happens by the thousands every day."

"It is amazing, that. A habit acquired by heredity, perhaps, or a challenge to the dogged British courage—like thick tea and suet pudding."

She laughed at his similes. "It's not so bad as that. We manage very well."

"And it satisfies you," he enquired of the back of her head, "to know that one day you will slide from friendship with one of your young countrymen into an unexciting intimacy and know yourself married? Is that how one regards the future?"

"You write us off as altogether too phlegmatic. You may be sure that we have our moments, senhor."

She turned, not realizing he was so near, and her hair brushed his shoulder. He moved away, got out another cigarette and, after lighting it and taking a deliberate pull, said coolly:

"It is time we arrived at the object of my call here tonight. I cannot, in the circumstances, stay very long. What can I do for you, *pequena*?"

She would have liked to remain near the window and maybe gain some of the nonchalance of the breeze. But he was standing inexorably by the chair she had left, and all she could do was utilize the seconds before they were re-seated in an attempt to gain the impersonality she knew to be necessary. The digression had been delightful but unsettling.

Felipe himself was urbane and diplomatic, but he valued straightforwardness in others, so her approach had to be direct and as objective as she could make it. She braced herself and spoke without looking at him.

"Senhor, may I ask why, after welcoming an art dealer to the Palacio and allowing him to believe you were interested in his pictures, you gave so little attention to them?"

Ever so slightly his eyes narrowed. "So it is for Maybury you speak, not for yourself. I guessed correctly. You have tried in a weak, unpersuasive way to get him to leave the island, and this friend of yours has the injured vanity. His fine Tintoretto is ignored and he wishes to know why. Is it not?"

"Surely you can see his viewpoint? He came here expressly to see you and he feels you didn't give the picture a sufficiently thorough examination."

"So?" To his coolness was added sarcasm. "This rabbit of a man has enlisted you as his assistant salesman. You have told me already that you know little about pictures."

"Almost nothing. We could never afford good ones."

"Then allow me to repeat that this is not a good Tintoretto and I will have nothing whatever to do with it."

His reply was so abrupt and emphatic that she sat stunned for a moment. She had heard of collectors acquiring pictures merely by the name of the artist, but apparently Felipe was not one of those. Tintoretto at his glorious, effusive best he admired; anything less was not to be considered.

Would he have bought it had Corina pleaded with him? Would he ever look at Corina as he was looking now at Laurie, with hard, hawk's eyes and his mouth inflexibly compressed?

Her eyelids lowered. "Very well, senhor. In that case there's nothing more to be said. I'm sorry to have brought you back here tonight, but as you guessed what was on my mind, it was really up to you. Anyway, I apologize."

It was done. Cedric would stay in Mondego till Stella returned. He would gently blackmail the Senhora Alvares into acquiring the picture, after which Stella would rend Laurie, and Henry Fielding would be deprived of the quarterly sum which tipped the balance between penury and seeming luxury. Laurie had lost.

But for her father she would not have minded. She was tired of being Miss Bell, tired of the half-lies and subterfuge, of losing her own identity; and it was time Stella reaped the reward of her selfishness. But persistently she remembered her father; his plasure in the Venetian goblets which Stella's allowance had enabled him to buy, the plans he had for replacing the merely old-fashioned in his shop with the old and the beautiful. Above all, his belief in Stella—it would be hateful to have to destroy that. The poor darling would grieve.

Could she, in the last resort, be absolutely frank with Cedric? There was nothing else.

Felipe was saying, "You will pardon me if I leave? I have matters to arrange for the morning."

She accompanied him into the hall, kept her arms at her sides for fear he would take it into his head to atone for refusing one favor by bestowing another. Felipe's mouth to her wrist would be more than she could stand just now; his lightest touch would be pain.

With his fingers on the bolt of the door he paused and swept over her his keen glance. "Well, Miss Bell, I have disappointed you, have I not? I said I would help you and now decline to do that which you want very much." Another pause in which, it seemed to her, her heart beat heavily enough for him to hear. "You do want it very much—that I should be kind to your Cedric Maybury?"

"I did. But it doesn't matter."

"It means a great deal to you—that the young man should make a big sale?"

The breath shuddered treacherously in her throat. Oh, why did emotion always have to attack the voice? It left one so defenceless. "It means almost . . . everything."

A moment's silence. "Then, for you, I will again examine the Tintoretto." A harshness overlaid the usually smooth tones. "But I will not see Maybury. It shall be arranged—without your aid."

"Thank you," she said faintly, scarcely believing. "I'm so terribly grateful."

On the point of making some caustic comment he seemed to decide against it. Instead he bowed distantly and went without saying good night.

Bereft of strength, Laurie clung to the wall and stared at the closed door. She hadn't lost, after all. She had won—the first round, at least; all she had to do was hope with everything she had that at a second inspection the picture would appear worth the enormous sum asked for it.

With an effort of will she straightened and turned back into the lounge. Ought she to get in touch with Cedric? No, she could trust Felipe, once he had made the decision, to act immediately. There was a chance that everything would turn out all right. Everything but her own relationship with Felipe, and about that it didn't do to think. Yet she did think about it.

What had he concluded—that she had acted for Cedric because of that friendship he harped upon? It was untrue, but better he should think that than guess at even a grain of the truth.

But how wonderful it would be to be truthful to Felipe; to say, "I am the sister of Senhor Alvares whom you count among your friends." A dangerous path of conjecture, though, because it opened up possibilities which could never exist for Miss Bell, Richard's nurse. In any case, there was no ignoring the existence of Corina Queira, who was the daughter of the Conde de Garda.

It was wrong to admit to herself a love for Felipe; he was now and forever a beloved personality whom she shared with the rest of Villa Barreiro. She must get that very firmly fixed in her mind.

For a day or two it was much cooler than Laurie had known it before on the island. Instead of sapphire the sky had a light jacaranda hue washed over by a pinkish-white haze which diffused the usually concentrated heat of the sun. The morning mists were unearthly, turning the harbour and the outriggers in the bay into a mirage which might dissolve at any second. Among the trees, the milky vapour rose about two feet off the ground and hovered there till swallowed by the sun.

The cooler weather was a boon to those effecting repairs to houses and gardens. It also brought alive new batches of cicadas, which shrilly clattered their wings from branch to branch of the nut trees even in broad daylight. After the roar of the cyclone their monotonous song had all the beauty of vast relief.

On Sunday morning, before Richard awakened, Laurie climbed the little mountain behind the Casa. She was tempted there by the sudden appearance of irregular blue carpets of flowers visible from the house windows, and when she reached them, to find myriads of heavenly lilies, waist-high, she could not resist an urge to tackle the last steep lap and stare out over a hundred other such small mountains writhing with fertile valleys. She wished she had binoculars so that she could pick out those groups of huts which covered the big undulations and ran away into the shadows as far as the eye could see.

So this was a native reserve, this wild and splendid country coerced into fertility in small patches round the huts and in the valleys where silver streams twisted and cattle chewed with the ever-alert white egrets not far away. In the morning light the whole scene was not colonial Portuguese but purely African—as African as the great brassy sun which climbed over an eastern ridge and spread a golden veil over the grass.

The widest river down there was the Guarez, which was reputed to shelter hippo and crocodile. The tallest mountain—a modest fifteen hundred feet—was called Monte Domingo, because it was the seventh highest peak in the island. Domingo meant Sunday, Laurie remembered, and the mountain shimmered with deepest gold as if conscious that this was her day. The hills about here were soft and green, dusted with pink.

Some experiences are impossible to analize. That crystalline view of low mountains brought a physical but not unhappy ache to Laurie's heart which she could not have explained away. She only knew that in spite of the heat and pests, in spite of an occasional cyclone and all the restrictions of living on an island, she would willingly stay in Mondego for ever. Just then she would have made no stipulations, no reservations.

She got back to the Casa and Sofia took the breakfast rolls from the oven. The familiar morning smell pervaded the terrace, where the table had been set. Richard, still in his pyjamas, came round the corner of the house; he must have seen her approach from his window and run straight out.

"Laurie's been walking," he accused her. "I want to walk."

"You shall, darling, right after breakfast. Let's go and brush your teeth."

She stood him on the low stool in front of the wash basin in the bathroom and watched his grave efforts with the small soft toothbrush. He was growing up, insisting on doing things for himself, getting angry when a button would not push into its hole, and sighing with pleasure when his fumbling attempts met with success. Rather like the three-year-olds at the Hollinshead Home, except that they competed fiercely with each other and therefore passed from babyhood even faster.

She hugged him suddenly and he looked at her reprovingly, as if he had expected rather more restraint from Laurie.

"Kiss Bunny and Woofie, too," he said impartially, and suspended operations till she had complied.

Towards lunch time a messenger came from Porto Mondego in a luxurious but ancient car, similar to several others on this island where there were no traffic problems. He had a letter for the English senhora. The thin square writing was puzzling, and Laurie slit the envelope with the haste of foreboding. But all she read was:

"Dear Laurie Bell:

Before the weather becomes hot again, I am arranging a picnic up the river, and I should be delighted if you and the small Richard will join us. There will be two other children and we shall take servants to see that the little ones are safe. We shall start from here on Tuesday morning at ten. It will please me so much if you can come."

The signature was that of Corina Queira. Coming from a Portuguese the tone of the note was distant, but Laurie recalled Corina's almost perfect English, the fact that she had been married to a surgeon and at one time had even considered a breakaway from the tradition that women were only housewives and ornaments, and training as a doctor herself. She also recalled that Felipe considered the woman too beautiful to be a doctor.

She wrote a note of acceptance and saw the messenger on his way. For the hour or two of siesta she could not oust Corina from her mind. She looked out a white frock which had pastel blue cuffs and collar, and powdered her hat with French chalk so that it would only need brushing before wear. Her shoes were starch-white and elegant; too elegant for a picnic, but the Portuguese dressed fashionably whatever the event.

She made some tea, and Sofia, when she rose from her couch, grumbled in a pleased way and permitted herself to be edged into a chair near Giulio's to enjoy it. For an English girl this Miss Bell was *simpatica,* Sofia thought; she had the quiet composure of the old Marqueza, who also had been English—but gay and spirited when young. This girl was like a pretty white lamp, waiting to be lit.

An hour later a second messenger, this time a donkey boy in a bamboo cart, pulled up his diminutive steed outside the Casa Margarita. The envelope he proffered was creased and dirty; he had it since sunset yesterday from the Senhor Inglez in Porto Mondego, who had paid him well to deliver it early this morning. But the senhora would understand that it took time to get from Porto to Villa Barreiro in a donkey cart. He had started, and then it came time for siesta, which one must miss no more on a Sunday than on any other day . . .

Even had Laurie understood she would not have been capable of according him much attention. For this note gave the news for which she had been so desperately longing.

Felipe had bought the picture. Cedric had the cheque—"You'd swoon to see the figures on it, Laurie!"—and he thanked her profusely for the word she had put in for him. The picture had sold itself, of course, but *she*, "his darling Laurie, his lucky piece," had enabled it to do so. He would never be able to put into words his gratitude, but she must know how he felt.

In a turmoil of thankfulness she gave the boy a tip and carried the grubby epistle to her bedroom to read again. Cedric would go home and everything would be safe: her father's allowance, her own position . . . everything. And Felipe would have the Tintoretto.

Would he remember, when it was placed in his gallery and he took guests along to look at it, that it was she who had begged him to give it the second examination which had prompted him to buy it? If so, she had planted just a wee bit of herself in the Palacio, which had its niche in his heart.

Would he let her see it when it was hung? He had never yet taken her to his gallery, never shown her the ancestral portraits, nor the beautiful one of his patrician mother. Laurie had no notion at that moment that she would visit the gallery in the Palacio the very next day.

CHAPTER ELEVEN

THIS WEEK, Laurie learned on Monday morning, was to be one of gaiety and excitement. From Wednesday, for three days, there would be *torneios* in which the young men would demonstrate their skill and audacity, and next Saturday the year's greatest *festa* would take place. Every night one or other of the bigger houses would be holding a *pateo* party, and there would be moonlight merriment on the beach as well. Villa Barreiro would hum with guitar music and song, with laughter and the sounds of dancing.

Had she a command of Portuguese, Laurie would have heard all about this much sooner. Sofia had mentioned it but not with the degree of enthusiasm usually accorded to the most important festivity of the year. Sofia was old, though, and past singing and dancing.

On the beach that morning, Laurie came across a group of young women, of whom Isabel Gourros was the centre. With their customary effervesence and kindness they hauled Laurie into their circle and asked what she intended to wear next Friday at the finals of the *torneis* and on Saturday at the *festa*. She shook her head and smilingly indicated Richard.

"But of course you will go!" exclaimed Isabel. "Sofia will stay with the child. The old woman has an easy time with you—the way you cook and help in the house. You must see that she does this for you. Almeido has already said he will be your escort."

"That's charming of him. I'll think about it."

"But you must act! Make for yourself a *festa* frock, Laurie, and practice a little our dancing; we will teach you. It will be madly exciting, I tell you, and who knows, someone may propose to you!"

"I would hate that."

Most of the girls knew no English, but they must have caught the meaning of this remark, for they stared incredulously and burst into astonishing laughter.

One of them said wonderingly, "You are droll, Laurie, and not to be understood. They say the Senhor Inglez wishes to marry you, and Almeido Gourros would come if you beckoned. I would give much to have Almeido even beckon to me."

"He is only a man," stated his sister scornfully. "Come now, Carmelina, tell us about that great skirt you are making with the lace frills under the hem and the belt so tight you are like to burst. Me, I would rather breathe than boast that a man could span my waist with his hands. I should be content with his arm!"

The conversation was so light-hearted, so eager that Laurie joined in for half an hour. Although it was doubtful whether she would be able to be at any of the evening parties, she decided for fun of it, to make a full black skirt with tier upon tier of colored braid at the base, and a white peasant blouse to go with it.

On her way up from he beach she called at the modest general store overlooking the stone harbour to choose material and cottons, and later, when Richard was resting, she cut out the skirt and blouse, and did some tacking. But while she worked she thought, not of the coming weekend functions which she might, anyway, be unable to attend, but of tomorrow, which she would spend with the definitely upper class Portuguese at a picnic organized by Corina Queira.

She supposed she ought to feel honoured that Corina had invited her to a social affair. The woman moved in a small exalted circle to which it was a privilege to be admitted. From the little she had seen of her, Laurie was unable to form clear-cut conclusions; the demure beauty of the Senhora Quera one could not help but admire, but even allowing for prejudice it was difficult to see in her a true mate for Felipe.

Laurie, in the new extra-sensitive state engendered by her own feelings for him, saw in Corina a sauveness, a lack of spontaneity which could not be disguised from Felipe for ever. There was nothing barbed about her—she was too sane and experienced, too much the Portuguese aristocrat for that—but it seemed pretty obvious that she did want the Marquez de Velho Barreiro for a husband,

and she was going the level-headed way about getting him. Why, otherwise, would she now take the trouble to make the acquaintance of Felipe's godson?

For two years Corina had been an enchanting and perhaps wistful widow. Possibly for the first of those years she had lived in seclusion, after which she had gradually emerged, a free, young and beautiful young woman. Her attractions for Felipe were not difficult to assess. She had wider knowledge and a sounder intellect than most of her women compatriots, an ancestry to be proud of, excellent taste, and that Latin faculty for assuring a man, without words, of a deep desire to please him. Instead of the coquetry extensively used by Isabel Gourros and her like, she had a calm self-assurance which probably arose from the fact of having been married. There was nothing so potent as marriage, thought Laurie, to dispel girlish shyness and implant serenity.

On the other hand, she reflected, a cold hand at her heart, the impression Corina gave of being perpetually cool and self-contained might arise from a more disturbing cause. Had she and Felipe an understanding? Were they waiting till they should both be back in Portugal among relations and friends before announcing their engagement?

Laurie snipped off lengths of scarlet, green and yellow braid and pinned them into position on the skirt. How utterly foolish she was to worry about the possibility of Felipe marrying Corina. Of course he would marry one day, and whoever he chose could not be right, in Laurie's view. It might as well be Corina as anyone else, she told herself sternly.

She folded away the materials, got into a fresh strawberry pink frock and gave Richard an entertaining lesson, judging by his chuckles, on how to buckle his sandals. This hour of the day had its own peculiar flavor for Richard. After drinking some fruit juice and eating a biscuit or a small cake while Laurie had tea, he invariably took one of his wheeled toys for a walk. Laurie, on these excursions, was expected to keep a pace or two behind in order to maintain his illusion of solitary magnifence.

Today he chose to take Juppy, the elephant, and as she went down the gravel road behind him. Laurie heard him talking confidentially into the big, floppy ear in a mixture of unintelligible English and Portuguese. The Portuguese, picked up parrot-like from nursemaids and servants, he pronounced perfectly.

They did not branch off to the waterfront, but kept on along the road, making for the public tropical gardens which were peaceful and scented as the day waned and the breeze cooled. There were few people about. They passed a mule-cart loaded with thatching grass, led by an African boy who smiled widely. An Indian family, parents, grandparents and numerous small offspring, sat at the roadside awaiting some expected conveyance, and a big, colored boy sailed by on a vermilion bicycle. There was an African nanny cradling a sleeping Portuguese child, followed by a dejected-looking terrier. And that was about all, before the big car came into sight and Richard whooped his recognition of it. There were few cars in Villa Barreiro and none so opulent as this.

It pulled up, as Laurie's heart had told her it would, and in a second Felipe got out and came round to them, and cast a perfunctory smile at Richard. Yes, perfunctory, Laurie noticed; and then she glanced upwards and saw that not a vestige of the smile was left in the dark features. He had a cold, insolent look; his mouth seemed permanently twisted with distaste and he gave them no word of greeting. There was something new and iron-hard in his manner, too. Laurie did not like it.

"You have an hour to spare—you two?" he enquired, his tone curt. "Come, then. I have something at the Palacio which will interest you." He bent and lifted Richard into the back of the car and wedged the elephant in beside him. "Take care this Juppy does not escape, Ricardo. To me he has a wild and dangerous look."

No underlying fun in his voice; the comment was merely an automatic reaction to the child's presence. Laurie got into the front seat, leaving eighteen inches of space between them. With part of her mind she had looked forward with even more than her usual longing to this meeting with Felipe, to thanking him for his prompt and generous action after their talk. It would have been a relief to put into words some of the gratitude she felt at knowing her father safe from Stella's wrath, but meetings have a habit of differing from one's anticipation of them. She could find nothing whatever to say.

Nor did Felipe bother to speak except to answer a piped question over his shoulder. They swept down the avenue of magnolias, between the tall, sculptured portals and round the long, shady drive with the trees and gracious statuary on each side.

Here was the Palacio, reflecting flames from the late sun, and the splendid sweep of terrace which was reached from the tiled courtyard by means of wide, semi-circular steps. Felipe brought the car to a standstill and helped out his two passengers.

To the servant who instantly appeared he said, "Take the senhorito to Diniz and see that he is amused. On no account is the child to be left alone. Understood?"

"Sim, Senhor Marquez."

Felipe hardly gave the two time to move off before slanting his enigmatic and austere glance at Laurie. "I would like you to go with me to the gallery. Perhaps you," with an unmistakeable sneer in his voice, "can instruct me where to hang this Tintoretto which I have acquired from your friend."

"Senhor . . ."

But Felipe had gone slightly ahead, to push open one of the big double doors, and when he stood aside for her to enter the lage, mosaic-floored reception hall, his demeanor was so unrelenting that an odd constriction gained control of her throat, and she found it impossible to finish what she had started to say.

Almost abstractedly, he stopped at the carved table and took a cigarette from the gold box. With the unlighted cigarette between his fingers he gestured towards the staircase.

"Let us go up at once, before the light goes. It is very necessary," with a suggestion of sarcasm, "that we choose the best possible position."

He did not touch her as they mounted the wide baroque staircase. She had the mad impression that if he *had* touched her she would have been bruised. Her breathing was becoming painfully irregular with bewilderment and fright, and at the top of the staircase she turned with him blindly, first along a beautifully-ornamented corridor which gave access to one or two bedrooms, then through a great archway which led straight in to the picture gallery.

It was a very long, high room, with windows at each end through which delicately-wrought grilles were visible. The ceiling comprised a series of old panel paintings preserved by a varnish which gave lustre to the gilt work of the carved wooden framing. Upon the length of one wall hung male Barreiros in velvet and lace and various highly decorative uniforms, and their wives and daughters in glorious silks and jewels. But Laurie was given no time to inspect them, nor to flicker an eye at the landscapes, still-lifes and allegorical pictures by famous painters which hung opposite them. Felipe threw his cigarette down upon a narrow table and indicated a large canvas, about eight feet square, which leaned against the wall.

Laurie looked at it only cursorily. "So that's the Tintoretto, it's even bigger than I thought. I do wish to thank you, senhor."

"So you wish to thank me!"

No one else could have imbued six ordinary words with such needle-sharp satire. Laurie froze. What was he getting at now? She saw him scrape with the thin blade of a silver penknife at a tiny blob on the frame, and winced inwardly at the inexorable cruelty of those long, tensile fingers; yet fascinatingly she watched the economical delicacy of his movements, the complete elimination of the offending spot.

"You have not, perhaps, examined the detail of a Tintoretto," he said with an icy deliberation which seemed to mask a fire. "The creative genius of the man was such that he cared only for the chance to express himself—not for money. His brushwork was certain, his sense of color inspired, and in his portraiture he closely followed Titian. In this, a semi-religious subject, you will see how well the figures are disposed and how apt the background coloring. There," he pointed at the hairs of a bowed golden head, "is the detail of which he was master, and there . . . is a matchless expression of holiness."

His manner had so much in it of caged anger that she was unable to yield proper attention to the picture. The more she strove to understand what it was that made him like this, the more fogged she became, and the more terrified. She decided to twist away from the Tintoretto, to gaze up into a painted face which had the familiar high cheekbones and point of dark hair above the centre of a deep forehead, the dark eyes; only that man's eyes were openly smiling, not narrowed and glittering like Felipe's.

"Now that you have seen this Tintoretto," said Felipe at her back, "I should like you to tell me where to hang it. I feel it should be your privilege." Then with heavy mockery: "If I had also a portrait of you I would set aside a room for you and this thing I have bought from the *enganador* you love—and I doubt if I would ever enter that room!"

It was not the word *enganador* but the contempt with which he uttered it that told Laurie he was calling Cedric a cheat. She swung round, trembling.

"Why are you speaking to me like this? Why have you brought me here this evening?"

"I will tell you," he answered rapidly. "I brought you here because there is much you should know about this Maybury to whom you have given your heart. I have told you I could not decide whether he is a fool or a knave. I now know him to be both, and I intend that you shall be very much aware of it, also!"

He was close, those eyes sparkling like coals, his teeth very white as he bit out the words. Laurie's heart thudded right through her body and her eyes were large and staring. His anger shut them in, with the picture.

"You wish to thank me for buying this thing, do you not?" he demanded savagely. "You wish to express your gratitude, because he had promised that the commission on this sale would enable you to marry. Is it not? *Is it not?*"

He did not pause for her reply, but without warning jabbed out at the canvas with his right hand. The blade of the penknife sank in and ripped a great three-cornered gap across the middle of the picture. Laurie gasped and her face went ashen.

"Felipe," she whispered hoarsely. "That's a terrible thing to do."

His teeth were snapped together now, his jaw so tight that the muscle was visible. "Terrible?" he said in a voice of polished steel. "Terrible to tear a piece of canvas which has been daubed by one criminal and sold to me by another? *Por deus!* Did that imbecile believe that I did not know a Tintoretto when I see one?"

He said more in those dreadful metallic tones while his eyes blazed and his dark tan took the bronze flush of absolute fury.

"A fake?" she groped at last. "Did you know it from the beginning?"

"Of course I knew, and I did not even need my magnifying glass to prove it. I was disgusted, and had it been anyone but Maybury I would have had him chased from the island."

"But this is appalling. Why didn't you tax him with it?"

"Ah, why! That is what I ask myself, now that I know more things. He comes, and at once it is apparent that you and he are closely connected. Is he a trickster, I wonder to myself, or merely a tool? Before I can find out it becomes obvious that you have faith in him, the undiscriminating faith that a woman has for the man she loves."

"You were mistaken, I don't love him," she said weakly.

"No? Then what do they call it in England when a woman risks other friendships for one man?" The tide of violence was ebbing, leaving him cooler and incredibly distant. "If you are not in love with Maybury, why did you beg me with your heart in your eyes to look a second time at the picture?"

Was it any good offering only half an explanation? If she said, "He'd stayed here so long that he daren't go back without making a sale," wouldn't it sound lame and concoted? Nevertheless, she did say it, and she added on a rising note, "We've talked of Cedric many times, and you've never hinted that your dislike of him was based on anything like this."

"He was a friend of both you and your father. I would have spared you if I could. I asked you to send him away, in order that his frauds might be detected elsewhere, but you, it seems, were bewitched by his glib tongue and his fair good looks. Then you plead with me to re-examine the monstrosity. You tell me that it means everything to you that this swindler shall sell it. I am sorry for you,' he ended curtly. "It must be painful to discover that the person to whom one has given only tenderness is the worst kind of charlatan. Any blow to the emotions is hard to bear."

Laurie had to turn her back on that mutilated thing against the wall, and upon Felipe himself. There was nothing she could say to him which would not make the matter worse. But she had not taken many paces before he came beside her.

"I regret," he said formally, "to have had to give you such news."

"I was thinking of the cheque," she said dully. "I'll get it back for you."

"You cannot. It is already deposited here for transfer to England. Let your Cedric have his money. It is the least!" His manner had gone so stern and cold that his words hurt like cast stones. "I intend to extort a promise from you in return for that cheque. The English mailship will not call at the island for ten days and there is no other way for this man to leave. I want your word that you will not see him during that time."

Her shoulders lifted, hopelessly. "How can it matter?"

"I am not arguing," he said sharply. "I am demanding that in this you obey me."

With sickening clarity it came to her that she could not obey him. There were things she had to impress upon Cedric, and she must give him a carefully-worded message for her father. Besides, distance altered one's perspective, and how could she be sure that back in England he might not regard her injunctions as far-fetched and rather funny? She really must be sure of his discretion; otherwise all she had endured just lately would be wasted.

"I wish I could do as you ask," she said, distressed. "I'll gladly promise to see him only once, for ten minutes."

Felipe's hand gripped hard upon her arm, just above her elbow. He spoke with an inflection so alien that dread again quickened her heart.

"The British loyalty, *ha?* Maybury is the dear friend, therefore any wrong he has done is necessarily a mistake. You will condole with him, assure him always of your friendship!"

"He's going, senhor, and I may never see him again." The eyes she raised to him held both pleading and pain. "Please believe that I'm insisting on this only because I have to."

"I will believe nothing," he said, "except that you are as infatuated with this man as ever. There is nothing to gain from further discussion. Let us go, Miss Bell."

Wordless, she walked at his side, down the length of the gallery, out into the corridor and down the staircase into the hall. The door stood wide, permitting the entry of a bar of bright light whose edge tipped with saffron the great sheaf of white flowers which stood in a metal bowl on a pedestal at one side of the entrance.

"One moment," he said distantly. "Wait here while I collect the child."

Vast as the reception hall was, Laurie felt stifled. She went out to the courtyard and stood there, looking down over the vivid gardens teased by the evening breeze. She could hear the fountains and smell jasmine, and in a minute or two she stood back and faced the house, absorbing the flamboyant grace of the Manueline exterior. She looked passionately as if to memorize for ever something she would never see again.

As though to confirm her foreboding, a car came around driven by a chauffeur, and at the same moment Felipe appeared on the terrace, holding the hand of his knee-high godson. There was an atmosphere of finality about the way in which he saw them seated, and the decisiveness with which he snapped shut the door.

"Adeus, Ricardo," he said. And then: "Goodbye, Miss Bell."

The car slid between the gardens towards the drive, and to Laurie it seemed that the whole of life itself was speeding away backwards under the wheels, never to be recaptured.

She recalled the violence of his anger over the Tintoretto—which wasn't a Tintoretto—those fingers holding the silver penknife as one might imagine a surgeon would handle a scalpel, the unleashed cruelty with which he had destroyed the canvas, which tomorrow would probably go on to a bonfire.

All hopes of true friendship with Felipe were gone. He despised her almost as much as he despised Cedric, and there was nothing whatever she could do about it. She sat tensely, trying with all her will-power to suppress the shivers which persisted in running along her spine.

CHAPTER TWELVE

NEXT MORNING Laurie awoke feeling so thickheaded and wan that her first inclination was to send an apology to Senhora Queira. She got out of bed and swayed to the window, gazed for quite a while at a very distant slice of blue-grey sea, and decided that it would be better, after all, to have something to do which would demand a degree of concentration upon pleasing others. Here, she could only mope, and remember.

How on earth had it happened that she, Laurie Fielding, had become so inextricably mixed up with these Portuguese? She should have stayed outside them, or made her friends only among such people as Isabel and Almeido.

Laurie sighed, pulled on a wrap and went to the bathroom. She had to get into a picnic mood, the mood in which one laughs through the day and pretends with gusto an unprecedented enjoyment.

A couple of hours later Pedro drove them into Porto Mondego; Laurie in the white with pale blue collar and cuffs, and Richard wearing a beige and tan suit which was inappropriate but identical in style with those worn by all well-bred little Portuguese boys on social occasions. Only peasant children went comfortably clad at all times.

They were received in the drawing room of the rambling Queira villa by Corina herself. Corina, sparkling in gay striped silk and yellow sandals, the heavy gold gipsy rings in her ears adding a touch of youthfulness to the sophisticated black hair drawn back from a centre parting into a loose but impeccably tidy knot. Her pale olive skin glowed and so did the deep, dark eyes. As hostess she was apparently in her element.

She made some introductions, and the other young women smiled politely while their men bowed and looked again at the English girl with the brown-gold hair and misty grey eyes. Richard was mussed over, even by Corina, who did not strike one as being truly fond of children. He loved it when they laughed at him, and showed off by gabbing nursery rhymes in both languages.

Lemon tea and home-made biscuits were served, and at length the company—about twenty in all and very restrained—trooped out to the waiting cars. Laurie and Richard were placed with a Senhor and Senhora Paixas and their five-year-old pudding of a daughter of whom Richard took not the slightest notice.

The twenty-five miles or so to the river were the most tedious Laurie had ever travelled. The car, third in a procession of four, bumped slowly over the rutted road and was oven-hot. Her adult companions made stilted conversation. They seemed to have concluded that she was clever and her career an original one such as was to be expected of the eccentric English. And how forward Richard was for a boy not quite three; the words he knew, and his intelligence! And so on, till Laurie drooped.

When the cars pulled up in a clearing beside a still, dark river, she revived a little, for this might be the mysterious hinterland of Africa itself. The grass had recently been scythed by Corina's own garden boys, and African servants had gone ahead this morning with folding tables and chairs which were now set up in the shade of the wild palms, creating a small civilization in a glorious wilderness.

Except for the clearing, which the island people themselves had made by felling trees and persistently keeping back the jungle growth, the river was walled in on both sides by tall mahoganies and coconut palms and the abundance of lesser vegetation which will always spring up where there are warmth and moisture.

Looking down the river from the water's edge was like peering along a green tunnel. There were trees with grotesque pronged roots that raked out into midstream, gigantic rubbery leaves lying on the black, treacly surface and, right down there near the bend, the gargantuan nostrils of many hippo just showing above the water. Laurie stared about her and up at the metallic strip of sky and was glad she had come, even though there were too many mosquitoes. Thank heaven it had occurred to her to dose Richard with paludrine and dab an oily repellent over his skin.

"Come," said Corina, "we grown-ups will play cards while the three children have lunch; it is best to give them their meal first in order that we may enjoy our own, free of them. Do you play bridge, Laurie?"

"I'm afraid not." It was too silly to bother with bridge in these surroundings. "This is new to me. Do you mind if I just look around?"

"But, no, if you find the river so worth looking at. Be happy in your own way, *minha cara.*"

It was the endearment which made Laurie pay closer attention to Corina? Was she imagining that the woman had a new, vital sparkle, the controlled gladness which might be part of such a woman when she knows herself needed by the man of her choice? There was nothing else in Mondego that could do this to Corina. Presently, the thoughts crystallized into fears, for she heard someone say—in English, because it would have been impolite to use Portuguese within Laurie's hearing—

"So Felipe was unable to come with us today? I had looked forward to being in his company."

To which Corina replied with a little laugh in which echoed a hint of excitement, "Had you not heard? Felipe will be away for three days. He has flown to the mainland to make some arrangements. Last night he dined with us—with Tio Luiza and me—and together we decided he should make this trip. No, do not ask me more," with a playful but firm shake of the head. "You will know all when Felipe returns."

Laurie moved away and the conversation proceeded in Portuguese. There seemed to be much staccato conjecture, many smiling denials from Corina. None of them suspected that Laurie, who was still seemingly intent upon the river, had gone completely numb.

Her first coherent thought was the reflection that last night, soon after the scene in the gallery, Felipe had taken his charming self—not the self he had shown to Laurie, but the one which never varied for Corina—to the Queira villa. Laurie had not even slipped into the back of his mind; she had gone from it altogether.

He and Corina had made plans. Plans for what? An engagement? A wedding in Portugal? She couldn't admit the marriage, Corina in his arms, the delicious domestic intimacy those two would share . . . everything. But not yet. The shock of new knowledge added to yesterday's experience was already too much to absorb. She felt buffeted and shaken.

The sun poured across the tree tops, the Guarez River lay enigmatic at her feet and monkeys chittered in the branches not far away. Yet the island was bleak and untenanted because Felipe had gone. Felipe, who was considerate and exquisitely courteous, impetuous and cruel . . . and infinitely lovable. The man she had crazily permitted to pervade her whole existence. He had gone, without her being aware of it.

When tea was prepared Corina came and sat beside her.

"Richard is an excellent example of how a child should be," she said, with that baffling smile which Laurie was beginning to loathe. "I am jealous of you, Laurie."

Jealous! If Corina only knew. Laurie could have laughed and wept. Corina meant she was jealous of Laurie's experience with children. She was thinking ahead to the time when she and Felipe would have a nursery of their own, when she would have to train a child and select a nurse. What a heart-wrenching thought that was!

"What made you choose to train in child care?" Corina wanted to know.

"I think it was the fact that . . ."

Laurie broke off suddenly, realizing with an electric stab of fright that she had been about to say, "I think it was the fact that Stella had taken up nursing." She had admired Stella and always loved children, so child nursing had been the natural choice. But to make such a statement to Corina! She really must take hold of herself, or she would find irretrievable errors hurrying from her lips."

She drew a breath past the obstruction in her throat. "I wanted to be a nurse and liked children," she stated in a colorless tone.

"Tell me about this Home in England where you were working. It is the sort of place of which we need many near the cities of Portugal. The convents are good but there are many little ones who need medical care and nursing."

So Laurie talked, apparently lucidly, for Corina nodded and put questions as if the subject really did interest her. The tea came, a weak infusion served in glasses and flavored with mint, and when it had been drunk and more politely jovial conversation had taken place, Corina gave the servants the signal to begin packing away.

A man asked if anyone present would be attending the *torneios* in Villa Barreiro. He was answered by languid disclaimers; *torneios* were the sport of peasants.

"Now the *festa* on Saturday—that is different," declared Corina. "The whole island will be in *festa,* and it is time, too. Gaiety is good for the nerves, particularly after such a cyclone as we had last week. Felipe is giving an open cocktail party on Saturday for any of us who wish to go to Villa Barreiro. I hope so much that you will all be there. You, too, Laurie. You have not yet seen Mondego in *festa.*"

Laurie smiled some reply. She was deathly tired of this picnic and these people, and all she wanted at the moment was to be back at the Casa Margarita with Richard. Perhaps, after all, Felipe's absence from the Palacio would be something of a relief. At least she would be free, for three days, of the acid-sweet fear of encountering him.

After a quiet day on Wednesday—quiet, that is, except for the shouts which came on the breeze from the square, where the preliminaries of the tournaments were taking place—Laurie went into Porto Mendego on Thursday morning to see Cedric. She could shirk it no longer.

It was not a painful interview. With the money winging its way to England and very few pictures to be packed for the return journey, Cedric hadn't a care. As the heat was still tempered by winds off the sea, and his luck at the Casino remained moderately steady, he felt he had no more to demand of the gods. For one more week he would bathe, dance and mildly gamble, after which he would go back to England to collect his nice fat spot of commission.

"I'd rather you were going with me, though," he told Laurie, as they sat over iced drinks in the Carnac lounge, "but I suppose that would be somewhat of an overflow of good fortune."

"I'm afraid so," she agreed. She had decided to be cool and to the point. "How soon after you get back will you be seeing my father?"

"I'll try to get up there within a few days of landing. I owe you that much."

"You'll tell him I'm happy here, won't you? Just say that Stella was away but you saw Richard and me. I'll write him about it, too."

Cedric looked at her sceptically. "You don't appear happy to me. To be honest, I'd rather tell him you're thinner and peaked-looking, and that his elder daughter goes in for sharp practice."

"But you won't," she said evenly. "You know that would break his heart."

He leant his arms upon the table and started at her. "What are you getting out of this, Laurie? You don't belong here any more than I do, and if your sister won't accept you as her equal there's no place at all for you. I think she's a horror—and that you're every kind of an idiot."

"You don't understand and I can't explain. But I want your promise, Cedric. My father musn't know that I'm called Miss Bell—nor must anyone else."

"I promise," he said resignedly. "You can depend on me."

"I think I can—mostly. But I have to be sure."

He gave her a nettled grin. "Not too complimentary, are you, darling? Haven't I behaved with the utmost circumspection?"

She nodded. "Yes, you have—because the Marquez forced you to. At first your anxiety was to keep in favor with him, and now you have immense respect for the man who bought your Tintoretto." She thought of something and added, "By the way, when he sent you the cheque did he forbid you to come to Villa Barreiro?"

"How did you guess?" he said lightly. "One could hate the man if one didn't respect his integrity . . . and his bankroll. If he hadn't been so emphatic about my staying away from that side of the island, I'd have brought the cheque for you to see. It was the most fabulous document I've ever handled and the signature was a honey."

"You didn't see Felipe at all, did you?"

"No." He paused, considering. "That part of it is something I've never made out. In all the time I've been on the island—it's getting on for six weeks now—I've only seen the man twice; the day we both met at the Palacio, and the following morning. For some reason," obviously unfathomable to the extrovert Cedric, "he took a dislike to me, but fortunately he was constantly in touch with you. Laurie, I've never properly thanked you for getting him to take another peep at the picture. I don't know how you managed it, but I'll be eternally grateful. You know that."

Laurie took one of the cigarettes from the packet he had opened and placed between them; she was smoking too much lately, but somehow it helped. She leaned to his match and lay back, inhaling. Was it better. after all, to leave the matter as it stood? Would it be enough to trust in his eternal gratitude? She was afraid not. The commission, in his easy fingers, would eventually disappear, and presumably his gratitude with it. Besides, he ought to be warned about those employers of his; if they tried any more tricks he might land in court.

Tentatively she asked, "Have you ever suspected the firm you work for?"

"Of what?"

"Of cheating their clients."

"Good heavens, my sweet innocent, it happens every day—only one doesn't call it cheating. One obliges one's clients. Someone wants a good old Sheraton table and you haven't got one, so you take one which has been made by a craftsman up the road, expose it to ageing devices and there you are!"

"Is that really so?"

"It does happen, my pet."

"Do you approve?"

"Come, now," he jollied her. "No one loses. The present-day craftsman is every bit as good as the old one and his tools are better. The customer is happiest of all because he's got what he wants."

"He's happy till he finds out that what he's bought isn't a genuine Sheraton." She spoke with cool sharpness. "Cedric, did you know the Tintoretto was bogus?"

Her answer was in his utter blankness, the visible drop of his jaw. "That can't be so. Of course it can't. Who told you?"

"Felipe. He knew it weeks ago, the moment he saw the picture."

Cedric had lost color and poise. "But it was insured in England for thousands of pounds. I still have my copy of the cover note."

"That was evidently part of the deception."

"Great stars," he said soberly. "I've been travelling around with dynamite." Swiftly, he braced himself. What's he going to do?"

"Nothing. In his opinion fraud always catches up with a person and you'd have to pay for it sooner or later."

"But the money—why should he part with that?"

A trifle wearily she knocked ash from her cigarette and dropped back against her chair. "Money isn't important to Felipe—maybe because he has so much. I didn't have his permission to tell you the picture was a fake, but it seemed to me that it might be good policy—for my own sake."

"I see." That he did see was patent in his next remark. "Astute of you, Laurie, but it isn't necessary. I wouldn't have given you away."

"I didn't really believe you would, but perhaps you'll realize now just how much it means to me that you keep anything you've learned here to yourself. Better still, forget it, as I shall try to forget the fake."

He bridled. "I shan't forget the fake! The damned cheek of it, sending me halfway across the world with a packing-case full of high explosive. I might have been thrown into some foreign jail! Once I get to Mauritius I'll travel by air. I'm just aching for a showdown with that crowd who sit back there and take the money while we others go out and risk our necks. I shouldn't be surprised if they owned both the original and the copy of that picture, so that they could pin the whole thing on me if it were found out!"

His anger washed over Laurie, leaving her untouched, except that she envied his resilience, the knack of assimilating news and leaping at once to his own vantage point.

She finished her cigarette, half-listening, and when he seemed to have ended, she said, "In your shoes I'd inform the police and let them deal with it." A pause. "I shan't see you again before you sail, Cedric. This is goodbye."

He smiled at her with sincere contrition. "My coming here hasn't done you any good, has it? It's worried and frightened you, but I'm sure you realize that that wasn't my intention. I'm fond of you, Laurie—and I always shall be—but I'm not nearly good enough for you. Will you believe me when I say I wish I'd left Mondego when you first begged me to go?"

"I'm afraid I wish the same." Had he gone then she might still count Felipe as a friend. "Do you sail a week today?"

"No, on Wednesday. Laurie," his hand moved across the table to cover hers. "I've got a silver cigarette case for you, just to show a little appreciation for all you've done." He tacked on hastily, "It wasn't bought with tainted money—I haven't collected any yet. Will you take it . . . please?" Her hesitation prompted him to belittle the gift.

He drew the small flat tissue-wrapped case from his pocket. "It's tiny and inexpensive, but I want you to have it and keep it. Drop it in your bag, and when you get home put it away till you can think kindly of me."

"I shall probably give up smoking shortly," she said. When Stella comes back, she thought.

"You won't now you've started—not in this climate. Please accept it, Laurie."

It was easier to take the thing than to start an argument. She opened her bag and let him slip the packet inside. "Thank you, Cedric," she said, and stood up.

Their farewell was almost formal. He saw her to the car, grimaced through the back window at Richard who was scrawling over a picture book with red crayon, and closed the door after Laurie had got in beside the child. The beige care purred out on to the Esplanda, Laurie waved a hand to the familiar figure of the only Englishman she had met in Mondego, and sped away from the town and out of his life.

It was like closing a chapter in her own life, too, except that there seemed to be no new opening to turn to, nor any hope of one.

CHAPTER THIRTEEN

PEDRO, PROBABLY for his own amusement, drove them back from Porto Mondego to the Casa Margarita by way of the big square in which the *torneiadors* were competing at odd hours of the day when they could be spared from their work at the harbor or in the plantations. Giulio was there, sitting on the low circular wall and watching a fencing match between two youths. His beret had taken an angle it would never have dared assume had his wife been near, and he smoked the smelly old cob pipe on a long stem which Sofia abhorred. He was defiantly enjoying himself.

The car crawled round the square, avoiding donkey carts loaded with bunting and dismembered food stalls, By tomorrow evening all the stalls would be erected and bunting flying between flag poles. There would be an abundance of highly-colored edibles for sale, a band parading, brightly dressed men and women in the streets creating an atmosphere of heady anticipation of Saturday's *festa.*

Laurie loved and envied the gaiety of these people. When sorrow came they steeped themselves in it; their grief was shattering but brief. Their joy was equally comprehensive, but they clung to it and relived it again and again. There were exceptions, of course. Like Sofia, who felt that the old days had been more full of incident, more romantic and vastly to be preferred to the present. To Sofia there was little worth striving for nowadays.

When they arrived back at the Casa the old woman was grumbling. "I need mangoes and corn cob for the lunch but there is no one to pick them. Those natives have finished their cleaning and washing and gone. Why, one asks, is that Giulio paid money for work he does not do!"

"I'll get them for you," said Laurie. "How many and where from?"

"Why should you do that which is his duty? I know where he is, that lazy old man. He watches the *meninos* rope the bulls and fight one another in the square. Always he snatches the excuse to waste time. And I here, needing the fruit and vegetables!"

"The *torneios* are only held once a year," Laurie coaxed her. "We saw Giulio just now, and he was in heaven, rocking himself backwards and forwards on the wall while the young men fenced. If you had seen him, Sofia, you couldn't have denied him such pleasure."

Sofia's stern old face was unrelenting, but her voice lost some of the harshness. "He is a boy still, my foolish Giulio. He watches and is again in his youth, when he could fight anyone and win. Yes, he is a boy still."

"There's a trace of boyishness in all nice men, and you should be glad that he has it," said Laurie, in Giulio's defence. "You ought to go with him, Sofia."

"I?" She shrieked her horror. "To the *torneios?* If they held them here in the garden I would not move from the house to see them! Those young men strutting out to demonstrate their stupid courage to the girls."

"Just as Giulio used to show his pluck for you!"

The old woman shook her head. "I thought you had more sense, you English, but perhaps one should not expect too much wisdom from the young of any country. You have heard that Almeido is to ask you to wear his favor at the finals tomorrow?"

"No—but I shan't be going to the finals."

"Why should you not go like other girls? The matches begin at four. You can take the little one until his supper time and go back later."

"Noise and excitement are not good for children."

"Phut," said Sofia. "Then you will leave the child with me."

"And you," said Laurie with irony, "are the one who has such contempt for the *torneios.*"

Sofia would not retract. "I still say it is madness to risk the life in order to capture the admiration of girls, but ever since the old days in my country men have always loved excitment and danger. One cannot stop them, so one must enjoy their performances or stay away from them. You have few happy times, senhora. You are too quiet, too deep in this matter of looking after Richard, when you yourself should be choosing a husband. Almeido is our most educated and prosperous *solteiro,* and I must say that his conduct in every detail is correct; he has the fine feelings, the wordly knowledge. You would not wish always to care for the children of others, would you?"

Sofia had the forthrightness of the women of her race about such matters. They made no secret of wanting a husband and children, and here in the island there were none who could be classed as spinsters because men outnumbered them.

Involuntarily, Laurie remembered that she had omitted to plant out the basil. In her present mood the caring for a plant and the wearing of a favor at the tournaments seemed childish, mere playing at love. She never encouraged Almeido even to step inside the gate as he came up from his office each afternoon, and privately she thought the young man kept up the gentle pursuit not because he wanted anything to come of it, but because she was different from the local girls and he wanted them to see that he, a travelled man, could appreciate another kind of woman.

"Come to the back," she said, "and show me which mangoes to pull."

Sofia vigorously shook her head. "The best are near the top of the tree and I cannot allow you to climb a ladder for them. We will not have mangoes. I will instead give you a lesson in one of the ways to serve canned peaches."

So Laurie helped her to make a salad of such ingredients as could be induced to grow in the moist heat of Mondego, and stood by while a caramel of peach juice and sugar simmered over the flame of a spirit stove. Sofia arranged the half-peaches round an oval dish, thickened the caramel with ground almonds, flavored it with lemon juice and cinamon and poured it over the peaches.

"We serve it chilled," she said, "with the sticks of sweet pastry. It would please me very much," she added with suspect ingenuousness, "if you would invite those two Gourros and perhaps another young man, for lunch or dinner. Not that I like that Isabel—she has a strong character of mischief and thinks she is free because her *apalavro* is in Portugal—but it is more discreet to have the sister with Almeido than one of the other girls."

"I don't think we'll bother, Sofia."

"We have not once had visitors for a meal!"

"The Senhora Alvares will be here in just over a fortnight, and I shall have to take Richard back to the Carnac. I'll give a farewell party."

"I will keep you to that word," said Sofia firmly.

Laurie smiled at her and went off to wash.

The unrest which pervaded the town could not by any means be excluded from the Casa Margarita. There was Giulio, who took a rating in the kitchen at lunch time but sidled off again during siesta. And there was Isabel Gourros, in a series of lovely frilly frocks and bright ribbons, breezing in on her way to and from the square to give the latest results.

"Antonio Parez is out of it, and I am not sorry! That one thinks too well of himself," she exclaimed. And: "You should see Henrique on a horse! He makes the heart to turn, that man. And he engaged to that thin-as-water Manuela, whose kiss would have as much fire as that of a mouse. One pities Henrique!"

No one would have believed that Isabel herself was betrothed to a sober horticulturist who was now completing a course which would enable him to take over important planting duties from the Marquez's bailiff; no one who didn't know her, that is. She wore the favors of two men; bunched them unceremoniously together and secured them at her waist. If either lost his contest she would toss away his emblem without a qualm.

Late that night a party was held down on the beach. From her bedroom window Laurie saw the camp fire sending brief paths of flame across the sea, and above the murmur of the waves she heard music and singing. It must have been well after midnight when a few merry-makers who lived in the houses beyond the Casa passed along the road; Almeido was singing in his liquid tenor, and Laurie judged, by the fact that he finished the song within her hearing, that he had paused for her benefit. In spite of herself she felt a throb of pleasure in being serenaded. They had some picturesque and endearing customs, these Portuguese.

After he had gone she got out of bed and drew back the curtain, and her breath caught in her throat. It was a scene of stirring beauty, the hill sweeping down to a sea shimmering with moonlight, the sky soft and warm in spite of the hard, brilliant sphere it cradled. Then and there she decided to spend an hour or two in the square tomorrow night, after Richard was in bed. She needed the fun. Heavens, *how* she needed it.

Next day she completed the eight tiers of braid on the black skirt and threaded a draw-ribbon through the embroidered loops at the neck of the blouse. Sofia dug out from among her unworn possessions a thin, gold-sequined belt which she pulled tight about Laurie's waist, and fastened.

When Laurie was ready that evening, the old woman came into her bedroom and stood back from her, critically.

"Do not draw the neck of the blouse so tight," she said. "It is permitted to show the shoulders, and you have the skin to entice a man's lips. Tonight you are a *menina,* like the other *meninas.* Almeido has not yet given you his favor, no?"

Laurie shook her head. "He's given me up."

Sofia smiled a small secret smile and said nothing. She stood indulgently in the porch while Laurie went along to Richard's bedroom, and when at last the slim figure came to her side, she touched the curling hair with a worn brown hand.

"Have good times and do not hurry back. And if you see my Giuilo, tell him not to come after midnight. He will be locked out!"

Laurie was one of the last to arrive at the square, and for a few minutes she saw no one she knew. Nor could she get anywhere near the circular wall inside which the events took place. Something was going on at this moment, for there were shouts of *"Holà!"* and *"Outra vez, amigo!"* and an occasional burst of clapping. A stallholder offered Laurie a chair.

"Stand upon it," he bade her in Portuguese, and then, realizing she was the English senhora from the Casa Margarita, he begged her pardon and requested that she follow him. Roughly, jestingly, he thrust aside the onlookers. "Make way, there, you clumsy peasants! The small senhora cannot see through your hides."

The crowd parted good-humoredly, and Laurie found herself standing behind the single row of chairs which surrounded the ring and seated the older senhoras, in their mantillas and sober Sunday gowns.

She witnessed the end of a display of horsemanship and a competition in gymnastics. Next came a short and comical wrestling match by two overdressed opponents, and during the pause which followed a gust of excitement ran through the audience. People murmured appreciatively. Now one would see things!

Laurie gathered that this was the highlight of the finals: a tussle between two young men and two bulls. The first to seat himself on the back of a bull and drop a garland over one horn would be the winner.

There is something in the composition of the Portuguesse which cannot resist the matching of man's strength with that of a bull. They have an affection for the animal but will not be mastered by it, as is shown in their bloodless bull-fights. The Portuguese bull-fighter would be ashamed to draw blood from a beast, let alone kill him.

There was no bull-fighting in Mondego, but this event in the *torneios* was intended to satisfy the more robust instincts. Laurie did not want to stay but she was too hemmed in to get away easily. More lights appeared over the empty ring and the whole audience tightened up with expectation.

The two young men came into the ring, neither very tall but both broad of shoulder and narow-hipped; typical specimens of Portuguese manhood. They wore tight black trousers, and the swarthy one had a blue silk shirt. Almeido, olive-skinned like his sister, his dark hair trimmed low each side of his face and his lips smiling, wore a floppy white satin shirt. He was cheered unceasingly, but took little notice, for his glance had gone at once to Laurie; he must have known previously that she was there.

He came to the wall and, after bowing deeply and courteously excusing himself to the old senhora in front, offered a flower over the top of her black mantilla.

"You will wear it for me, senhorita?"

Conscious of a myriad of avid glances, Laurie smiled nervously, raised a hand to catch the flower but instantly drew it back. She had recognized the blossom—an opening oleander bud nestling in a spray of dark leaves.

"No, senhor," she said huskily. "I'm afraid I don't care to watch this kind of thing."

"Throw it to me, Almeido!" cried a daring voice. "I'll keep it cver my heart."

But he was not listening; his eyes were on Laurie's. "I implore you, senhorita," he said.

Her senses swimming, she replied, "I'd really rather not."

Then aloof, kindly tones broke in, from somewhere to the right and behind Laurie. "You embarrass the senhora, Almeido. She is not of us and does not comprehend that you are merely paying her a compliment. I am sure your good mother, the Dona Maria, will wear the flower for you."

Laurie's head was bent, but as her own spine stiffened she felt the stiffening of the crowd and heard pleased ejaculations. "The Senhor Marquez is here! How Almeido is fortunate to have the Senhor to watch his victory!"

Taking hurried advantage of the diversion she twisted and blindly pushed her way through the crowd. In the comparative outer darkness she turned swiftly to walk round the square, but the road was blocked to prevent the bulls from escaping as they were led into the ring. She shrank back against the railings, put both hands behind her and held on tightly to the iron bars.

Felipe was back. Her unruly heart took wings while her eyes wanted to weep for the little blow she had dealt Almeido. "Any flower but an oleander," she whispered aloud to herself, "and I'd have taken it." She hadn't known, till that moment near the ring, that she had regarded the oleander as her own flower, and Felipe's. How mad life was, how unexpected in the sharp obstructions it thrust up in one's path. A small waxen flower, whose leaves she knew to be bitter with a healing juice.

Felipe was over there, looking on at the happenings in the ring. Every one, even the stallholders, had pressed forward, and the shouting was frenzied but unintelligible. Laurie, close to the railings in the shadow of a tree, felt slightly sick.

What had Felipe thought of her refusal to wear Almeido's flower? Had he guessed at a reason that was anywhere near the truth? How strange that she had not felt him close before he spoke; but possibly he had only arrived at the square in time for the last contest. Yes, that was it; he had merely shown up for the look of the thing, the *grande calvalheiro* honoring the most important of the tournaments with his presence.

She wished she had seen his face, if only for a moment. She had a sudden hunger for a glimpse of him, tall, proud, coolly mocking, but now and for ever the man in her heart. Yet she could not bear the thought of his seeing her, because they were enemies, would always be enemies.

On the far side of the square was another exit which led off to the waterfront. It would mean going the long way home, but out there it would be mercifully dark and deserted. No; much though she longed to see Felipe, she longed even more for the anonymity of darkness.

Nerving herself, she started walking up the narrow pavement alongside the rails. On the left the unattended stalls were piled high with dishes of shellfish, sweet-milk *paozinhos*, foaming heaps of grated dried meat sprinkled with chopped nuts, olives, onions in pink vinegar, and dozens of varieties of sweets and pastries. There was a herb stall where lovers' posies and charms were for sale, and beyond it the mysterious tent of a fortune teller who sold love potions.

Love potions, thought Laurie hollowly. A spoonful of the mixture in a man's wine. If only it were as easy as that!

A shout went up. The *torneio* had ended, and there was no doubt as to the popularity of the winner. In her anxiety to be gone from the square before the crowds dispersed, Laurie moved faster. But the vendors rushed back to their posts and customers already began to select sweetmeats and savories, and to flip coins across the stalls.

She stepped down into the road, managed to wriggle through a laughing mass of people and was straightaway confronted by the panting Isabel.

"My faith, what a crush! I have been looking for you, Laurie. Please come. Almeido is hurt!"

"Hurt?" Laurie stared. "Didn't he win?"

"But of course he won!" Impatiently Isabel jerked Laurie's arm. "Though he is my brother I must say he was superb. But always he will demonstrate!"

Laurie knew that word, the way the Portuguese used it; it was a favorite of Sofia's. "Is he badly injured?"

"His arm is torn, near the shoulder. You are a nurse, Laurie, and you must help him."

"I thought it was usual to have the doctor in attendance. Isn't he here?"

"How you ask questions! The doctor was called from the square an hour ago to a woman who is very sick. There is a medicine box, and all you have to do is to dress the wound. We do not need the doctor." Isabel was dragging at her. "Almeido is over here in the marquee of the *torneiadors.*"

Laurie was running with her but still protesting. "I doubt whether I can do much. He probably needs medical attention."

"In Villa Barreiro we have only one doctor, and he is out, but you are the next best thing. Here we are. Come inside."

Considering that about forty people were crammed into the performers' tent, the place was singularly quiet. Laurie blinking in the sudden light, had reached Almeido's side before realizing the meaning of that quietness. Felipe was there, bending with some concern over the blood-stained upper arm. He was speaking softly in Portuguese, but when he became aware of Laurie's presence he changed to English.

"I saw the tip of the horn at your shoulder, my friend, but did not guess the extent of the damage. It is painful?"

"A very little, senhor," replied Almeido.

"More than a little, I think. We must stop this bleeding."

Isabel then curtsied and gasped prettily, "It was the bleeding which made me run to find the Senhora Ingleza. She knows much of these things. I have seen her bandage the native servant."

"So?" His glance barely touched Laurie, and he went on speaking to Isabel. "Hot water, *menina,* please. Ah," as someone pushed nearer the folding table with the medicine chest upon it, "it has a lethal look, this box of medicaments, but do not worry, Almeido. We will not amputate!"

Laurie did not look at him again. Her training came to her assistance, calmed her nerves and forced her to ignore the fact that it was Felipe who selected tweezers and wads of cotton wool. She smiled impersonally at the seated Almeido, took the longest pair of scissors from its compartment and snipped round the armhole of his sleeve. Felipe drew the sleeve down over Almeido's hand.

"Will you rip it up and make a tourniquet, senhor?" she said. "Just here, please."

After that, speech was unnecessary. The tourniquet was fixed, the wound, a jagged tear on the outside of the arm, was swabbed and painted with antiseptic. Felipe, with both hands cupped along the arm, held the edges of the cut together while Laurie, having found a roll of the new transparent medicated tape among the dressings, lopped off short lengths and applied them crosswise down the length of the deep, purpling wound.

Felipe held the pad of cotton wool in position while she bandaged. Almeido's mother, who sat throughout on the other side of her son, sighed something in Portuguese, and Laurie sensed a change in the atmosphere—a slight withdrawal of the spectators. But Felipe made no sign. His fingers were cool and steady when hers unavoidably touched them, and as she finished he handed her the scissors, and himself gradually removed the tourniquet.

She straightened, discovered that Almeido was looking at her strangely, and thought he had probably been looking at her like that for some minutes. Again she contrived the smile.

"Have you forgiven me, Almeido?"

He quickly averted his eyes. "It is for you to forgive me, senhora," he said.

The "senhora" put them leagues apart. It seemed to hold an echo of whatever it was his mother had murmured. Laurie turned to dip her hands into the bowl of fresh water and met a peculiar query in the dark eyes of Isabel. When she dried her hands they were quivering and her whole being had unbearably tensed. What was the matter with these people? She had done nothing but that which any other woman with similar training would have done, but they were behaving as if she had proved herself to be not quite human.

Almeido was standing now, and someone had placed a tray of drinks on the table. Felipe had handed a glass to the old senhora, put another into Laurie's hand and a third into Almeido's. He raised a glass himself, and slightly inclined his head towards Dona Maria. His manner had all the charm for which he was loved.

"A worthy contest, eh, senhora? The bull may have gored our Almeido, but he made the beast look very foolish afterwards, with a garland over one eye and a rider on his back. I have never seen such speed!"

The atmosphere eased. They drank with the quickness of accustomed wine drinkers, and Laurie set down her glass while it was still half full.

The tent was emptying, and outside the noise increased. Tonight, the people would eat a lot and sing; then some of them would go to their houses, while others stayed out into the small hours to welcome those who, even now, were driving in from their small mountain farms in order to be early on the spot for tomorrow's *festa*.

"My car is at the back of the square," said Felipe. "I will take you to your homes."

Laurie went ahead with the oddly quiet Isabel. When they reached the car the three women got into the back, and Almeido into the front seat beside Felipe's. They drove away from the square and up the moonshot hill to the villas above the sea. There was no talk on the way.

Felipe stopped at the gate of the Casa Margarita, opened the back door for Laurie, and went with her along the path to the lighted porch.

He bowed. "You have had a tiring evening. Drink some warm milk with whisky and go straight to bed." Laurie gave a barely perceptible nod, and he went on, his tone tinged with cold malice: "These love affairs are wearing, are they not? Almeido should have given you time to have done with the Englishman." He allowed her no retort, even had she been capable of it. His hand pushed wide the door. "Do not forget that whisky. Good night."

She entered the hall and closed the door behind her. She raked back her hair with a shaking hand, then saw Sofia standing in the lounge doorway, her expression one of jubilant anticipation.

Laurie squared her shoulders. It was not yet time to surrender to the utter despondency which filled her being.

CHAPTER FOURTEEN

LAURIE saw little of the *festa.* There were folk dances in the public gardens when she took Richard for his walk, and from the corner windows of the house it was possible to glimpse the crowds down at the harbor, but the main part of the *festa,* the eating, drinking, dancing and singing, was merely a muted roar to the inhabitants of the Casa Margarita.

Giulio tried to fit in some of the work he had neglected, but it was easy to see that his mind was still with the *torneios* at which, annually, he relived his youth with all the delight of his simple personality.

"You know, senhora," he said to Laurie at mid-morning when he sat under an acacia with his mug of chocolate, "I was the best horseman in Mondego. We had horse-racing then, and always I would win."

"And now you cannot even sit on a donkey without the backache," put in Sofia, who rocked in an old chair nearby.

He chuckled. Sofia's soliciting, even when she was at her most cantankerous, always left him unruffled, and it never upset him to be reminded that he was old. He talked of forty years ago when the population was much smaller and families vied with each other for the greatest number of points in the competitions. And he told of how he and his brother had married Sofia and her sister because they could cook.

"They were not bad-looking, you understand," with a patronizing grin at his wife, "but then a woman who can cook is never ugly. She has a soul."

"Which is more than one would say for the man who cannot resist a plate of food, whatever the hour," came the retort. "He has only the stomach!"

Laurie sipped her chocolate, hardly listening to the good-natured bickering. She felt flat and her brain was woolly through lack of sleep. Awakening much too soon this morning, to see the peasant skirt and blouse lying over the back of a chair where she had thrown them in her unhappiness last night, she had vividly recalled those minutes in the big tent and Felipe's sarcasm when he had said good night. She had seen him flicker over her dress a glance of distaste. What had he expected of her: expensive silk and a lace mantilla? She was angry with him for spoiling the pleasure she had had in making and wearing the clothes; and hurt deep inside, because that is inevitably the lot of the woman whose love is unwanted.

She had thought, and hoped, that Isabel would call this morning. Instead there had come a note from Dona Maria, stiltedly thanking the Cenhora Ingleza for the help she had given Almeido. The usual invitation which accompanied such a letter of thanks was missing, and Laurie knew there must be an important reason for the omission.

However, as the day went by without a single caller she blamed the *festa* for everything. Few people passed the Casa. Africans came by, bearing on their heads wide, flat baskets of fruit and other foods for which they had been sent by their masters, the stallholders. They were mostly stringy boys wearing only a *lapa* fastened about the waist and ornaments in their ears.

The day went tranquil for seista, which finished later than usual, possibly because the merry-making would go on well into the night, and was not likely to get under way till dusk. But darkness comes early and swiftly to the tropics. The sounds of revelry, of guitar, accordion and castanets, were plainly audible when Richard had his supper at six, but he slipped off to sleep as a child will, whatever the noise, if he is healthily spent.

With Sofia and Giulio up the road having their Saturday evening gossip in the room of Sofia's cousin who was maid to the schoolmaster, and the child away in the land of dreams, Laurie felt lonelier than at any time since her arrival in Mondego. Her book, which had promised to be diverting when she had started reading it a day or two ago, had gone flat and uninteresting; she had no desire to read, anyway.

She went out and sat in the dark veranda, was able to shut out the distant strains of collective joy, but was unsuccessful in her efforts also to exclude the Palacio from her thoughts.

Corina had implied that a party, invited by Felipe, would this evening grace the *festa*. Laurie supposed it was customary for the aristocratic element to join the dancers for a while; it gave the occasion an air which it would otherwise have lacked.

Corina and those others who had attended the picnic would now be driving up to the Palacio for cocktails. The place would be ablaze, the chandeliers scintillating, and innumerable uniformed servants would leave among the immaculate, white-clad men and bejewelled, silken women, serving drinks and the dainty canapés which whet the appetite. Presently they would get back into their cars and drive down to the square. And when they had spent an hour or two mingling with plantation supervisors, shopkeepers, fishermen and the rest, they would drift back to the Palacio for a very late dinner followed by sophisticated ballroom dancing, card games and much well-bred gossip.

Keenly, Laurie felt her own position. She was on the dividing line between the two classes, part of neither. She was beginning to think that it would be good to get away from Villa Barreiro and even to have Stella back. Before the Alvares went away again they would perhaps be able to rent a villa in Porto Mondego. Certainly she, Laurie, would oppose another spell on this side of the island.

The next two or three days passed quietly. It was a strange quietness, inexplicable when Laurie looked back upon last week and the chattering of the girls about the *torneios* and the *festa*. She knew from Sofia that they were meeting in one another's *pateos* and describing to each other their conquests. But none of them popped into the Casa Margarita.

Then on Thursday, as she pulled Richard home from the beach in his two-wheeled cart, Laurie met Isabel returning from an errand. They climbed the road together, Isabel taking half the handle of the cart. The Portuguese girl vivaciously described a swimming party she had persuaded her mother to sanction, but at the end of her recital she cast a sidelong glance at Laurie, and added smoothly:

"Tomorrow, several of us are going to Porto, to wish *bon voyage* to Senhor Maybury. Will you be there?"

Laurie shook her head. "I've already said goodbye to him. He'll be pleased to have you see him off, though."

Isabel shrugged. "We go just for the fun. My mother said you would not go."

"Your mother?" This was odd. Dona Maria had never before shown more than a perfunctory interest in any of Isabel's friends.

"She always makes much of the things she sees. She has not yet recovered from the way you bandaged Almeido, and she now thinks you are different from every other girl. I suppose she is right."

A question came into Laurie's mind, but she hesitated before casually voicing it. "Isabel, what was it your mother said that evening, in the tent?"

The dark eyes looked ahead, but Isabel had no reticence in her nature. "We young ones would not dare to say such a thing in front of the Marquez, but she is older and privileged. She said that you and the Senhor worked together on Almeido's arm as if his mind were yours, and yours his. And now everyone feels that we should not have asked you to our parties. The Senhor himself said earlier that you are not one of us."

"So I'm condemned to be cold and solitary because I'm not Portuguese!"

"Of course not. But it is true, is it not, that you have received invitations from the Senhora Queira?" Not waiting for a reply, Isabel added, "Me, I am not awkward with anyone, but the others are not like that. All have heard that you are friendly with the Senhor, and now comes poor Almeido's torn arm to show that you do not behave with the Marquez as we do. Even here on the edge of Africa one maintains a code."

More than that Laurie could not drag from her. Isabel's volubility had a glossy veneer of politeness which Laurie could not pierce. It seemed that even she was infected with this bug of correctness which it was impossible to eliminate.

So they had drawn conclusions—erroneous ones!—from her own problematical friendship with Felipe. ". . . as if his mind were yours and yours his." If only it were true! It sounded romantic, but all it really meant was that she and Felipe had shared a duty of which both had had previous experience. Obviously he had known what he was doing, and she, perforce, had co-operated.

What had he thought when he heard those words from Almeido's mother? That the people about him were villagers who loved extravagances of phrase, that the Dona Maria was to be excused because of her distress over her son's injury? Quite certainly he had shrugged off the comment as negligible. He probably wouldn't believe that it had left an impression upon others who had heard it.

It was typical of the way she felt that straight after lunch Laurie looked up Stella's last letter and worked out the length of time to go before her sister's return. Eleven days, which meant ten days here in the Casa and one for settling in at the Carnac.

A pity Richard had to go back to the hotel. The uneventful way of living suited him so well that the little smudges under his eyes were disappearing, and he had much more vitality. Except for the episode with the sting-ray she had not had to call the doctor to him, and for the next eleven days she must watch him even more closely and keep her fingers crossed. It would be too bad—and not only for Richard—if he caught a chill or picked up a germ at the last minute.

Would her life change, she wondered, when Stella and her husband were here again? She badly needed more social contacts, and she would give anything to meet someone whose interests lined up with her own. Here in Mondego, where one was surrounded by the gay and hospitable, it was possible to be horribly lonely. Even a knowledge of Portuguese would have been no guarantee that she would find close friends; and now she had no desire to find them.

It came to her, starkly, that the attractions the island had held for her were being dissipated by a positive shrinking from the prospect of remaining here, a paid appendage of Stella's and unwanted by anyone except Richard. Her heart turned fiercely from the idea of living where Felipe was not, yet to be near him was a torture she knew not how to endure.

What did one do when the man one loved was hopelessly out of reach? Wasn't it sense to get as far away from him as one could, and to put other things in his place? Sense, perhaps, but reason and the pangs of love are often irreconcilable.

There were fevered moments, which usually came when she was in the dark and alone and thoughts were difficult to control, when it did not seem such an impossible thing that Felipe should love her. They had talked together a good deal, had discussed the subjects men and women do discuss when they are equals and keen to learn more of each other, and had laughed at the same jokes. He had been kind.

But kindness, daylight had told her with cynical dispassion, was a coin that he dispensed liberally to every one with whom he came in contact. And she was not to forget his violence and contempt over the faked Tintoretto. Besides, said the mockingly brilliant morning light, Felipe may be the sun and the moon and the stars to you, but there's nothing to prove that you so much as flutter his pulse.

She was glad when Richard called that he wanted to get up from his rest.

Later, when the sun was going down, they took a walk from the back of the house, along a rough path which wound about the foot of the low mountain and led eventually to the native reserve. The African servants of the villas always used this footpath, which was why the fruit and nut trees on each side were denuded and many of the branches mercilessly hacked. Here, where the growth was jungle thick, the wild bananas grew extraordinarily tall and bore tiny inedible fruit. The ferns, too, were so lankly overgrown that they were caught up in the lower branches of the thin trees and laced together with vines.

Only little grey monkeys and hordes of insects lived in the bush. No one had ever seen a land snake on the island, though water snakes were known to breed near the larger rivers. Laurie never cared to penetrate the more dense parts of the mountain slopes with Richard, even though his skin was invariably protected against insect bites.

"Come, darling, we'll go back now," she said. "The monkeys are sleeping today."

He came out with his customary monosyllable. "Why?"

"Perhaps they played too hard this morning."

"Want to watch the fishes at the bridge," he said.

So they wandered back to the primitive little bridge made of stones and supported by boulders round which the clear waters curled, and she kept a safe arm about Richard while he sat with his legs dangling and became engrossed in his favorite occupation.

No one but natives needing water bothered to come to this stream, yet it was one of the loveliest Laurie had seen. Farther up, towards the bend, lilies stood out of the water, jungle lilies from three to five feet above the surface. Their spiky mauve trumpets were enormous, unblemished examples of tropic luxuriance. She was still brooding upon the beauty of the lilies above still water against a background of dark vegetation when Felipe came upon them.

He must have approached quietly, for the first indication of his presence was a cool and smiling comment.

"She has grace, the little Dominica. Did you know it is the same stream which runs through the grounds of the Palacio?"

Richard gave an ecstatic whoop. "Your fishes are best, Tio Felipe."

Laurie had a moment in which to collect her suddenly scattered wits. She lifted Richard to his feet, and had to take the hand which Felipe held out.

"I can't think why he's so obsessed with fish," she said, quite steadily in spite of the fact that Felipe's strength had drawn her to her feet and his firm hold had moved to her elbow.

"He will lose that obsession when he has seen a train. This bridge is too narrow for comfort. Come *pequeno*."

He hoisted Richard on to his shoulder and, gently pushing Laurie in front, got the three of them off the bridge and on to the path which led to the orchard garden of the Casa. With Richard on high, there was just room for two to walk closely abreast. But while Felipe took care that Laurie avoided rocks and roots in the path, it was to Richard he talked; about the wild orchids which unaccountably had rooted in tree-trunk crevices, about the bright little birds which always flew around in couples in hot countries and had many more families than the birds of cold lands, and about the monkeys which were certainly peeping between the leaves, though one could not see them.

Inside the garden he set the child down. "Go to find Sofia," he said. "She expects you."

Part of Laurie's mind noted how obedient Richard was; that, like his absorption in fishes, was a phase he would grow out of. The rest of her mind was occupied with the fact that Felipe had come today for a purpose. She didn't know which was stronger; her longing to be alone with him and hear what he had to say, or her dread of it.

They had slowed in the shade of a group of avocado trees and Felipe's fingers, which she was beginning to know as intimately as she knew her own, reached up to feel round one of the large, shiny green fruits. His thoughts, she was sure, were not with the action.

"Will you come into the house for a drink, senhor?" she asked conventionally.

"Thank you, no.,, He looked down at her, his regard light, quizzical and utterly aloof. "Your Cedric Maybury leaves tomorrow at eleven. You know that?"

"Yes, I know."

"It does not distress you?"

She shook her head. "Not a bit. I shall be glad when he's gone."

"How very sensible and English. To burn one's boats, make the clean cut—or what they may call it. The English are good at that."

"But even the English," she answered evenly, "are not always able to follow the dictates of common sense."

He nodded distantly but comprehendingly. "You, too, would like to make the clean cut? Can it be that there are things here in Mondego which unpleasantly stir your cold blood? For you, that would be a disaster, would it not?"

She saw him detach one of the avocado pears and press a dent into the tough skin with his thumb. He tossed the fruit into the soft earth at the foot of the tree, and looked at her, as if expecting some rejoinder.

She averted her head and replied to him with a non-chalance which nearly matched his own. "Through living here I've become inured to minor disasters. In time I shall also become hardened to other facts." A brief pause. "Why did you come here today?"

His smile was sharp and did not reach his eyes. "You are blunt, my dear Laurie. I am not accustomed to having to explain my right to call upon anyone living in Villa Barreiro. I came to see that all is well with Richard before I go away tomorrow.

Her heart gave a sickening lurch of which some sign, surely, must show in her wace. "Away?" she echoed. "Are you going to the mainland again?"

But she knew that could not be so. He was going for longer this time, or he would not have troubled to make this visit. A yearning impatience kept her teeth tightly clamped while she awaited his answer.

"Not to the mainland. I went across last week to make some arrangements for another trip—more protracted. This time I go to England."

England! Involuntarily, she stared up at him, but the fortitude which stiffens most women in moments of stress kept her expression almost blank, while her brain darted with anguished delight.

England with Felipe! The theatres and shops of London, the dark cliffs of Cornwall, the moors, the meres and dales of Northumberland. The simple things, like the wind over the heather and a brown field ridged with frost, a quiet, meandering river and a temperature cloud-strewn sky. All this and much more, with Felipe. Her lip turned in between her teeth and she bit on it.

"Which part of England?" she asked carefully.

"I shall stay in London, but will have to spend some time at the house which was my mother's. If I were English I suppose I would live there. As I am not, it is unoccupied, and I have to decide whether to sell it."

"You said the house was in the Cotswolds."

"It is one of your big, draughty mansions, with a baronial hall which is all dark panels and leaded windows, and great uneconomical kitchens and outhouses. As a child I had some affection for the place, but now," a characteristic shrug, "the ties do not exist, and it irritates me to think of the waste. Something must be done about it."

She had to ask: "Will you be gone long?"

"Only a month. I travel by air."

She had thought he might say two months, or even three. Yet now she knew that one month can be a lifetime. Laurie's throat had the tight, frightened feeling which comes with a shock to the emotions. Though why it should be a shock that Felipe was going away was hard to fathom. For a long time in the back of her mind she had known that he could not stay for ever in Mondego. He had estates and business interests in Portugal, where the climate was kinder and other branches of his family lived; she had never imagined his going to England, though.

They walked on together under the trees. The slanting sun created shimmering patterns of leaves on the grass and it shed pure gold over Laurie's bent head.

This was the last time she would see him for a month. Wasn't there something she could say which would turn the farewell into . . . into a half-promise? If only he would leave her something to cling to, a lifeline of hope. She stifled a sobbing little laugh. How astonished he would be could he read the ridiculous trend of her thoughts!

They were on the side path now, and mounting into the veranda. His car was out there on the road, the metalwork sending out shafts of fire in the sun. Seeing that he had refused a drink, Laurie thought he would say goodbye and go, but he opened one of the french windows and followed her into the lounge.

"There was something I wished to ask you," he said, standing with his back to the light and his hands behind him. "It occurred to me that you might like to send a message to your father. If you will tell me where is this little store of his I will deliver your message personally."

Afterwards, Laurie knew that it was those particular words of Felipe's which rocketed her back from the sphere of absurd yearning into cold sanity. When he spoke them, however, she was too dazed by the flood of implications to think coherently.

"It isn't necessary," she said swiftly. "I write to him by air mail."

"But you know how it is with parents," he persisted. "I believe there is a very real fondness between you and your father, and it would please him to meet someone who knows you here."

"York is a long way from the Cotswolds."

"It is much farther from Mondego. I would like to do it for you."

"But I couldn't let you."

Now, her brain was functioning more normally, and she saw the enorimity of his suggestion as *it* affected herself and Stella. The Marquez de Velho Barreiro in the little antique shop in York, discovering that the owner's name was Fielding, not Bell, and that Henry Fielding had two daughters, not one. It was unthinkable.

To lend a more casual air to her refusal of his offer, she went to her bag which lay on the table, and drew from it a handkerchief.

"My father is perfectly satisfied with the letters I send him. He isn't the worrying kind."

"Nevertheless, from what you have told me about him, I think he would appreciate this small service. I shall hire a car in England so it will cause me no trouble, I assure you."

Laurie had never thought it possible that that consistent courtesy of his could be so hard to wear down. The worst of it was the ache of longing to be able to do as he wished. She had to be hard about this, hard and firm. There would always be an insuperable wall between herself and Felipe; the wall created by her own acquiescene in Stella's deception; she must not forget that for a second.

"Perhaps you won't understand, but I'd rather you didn't call on my father," she said.

He had been watching her with a satirical shrewdness, and now he enquired abruptly, "You have a reason—one which you prefer not to tell me?"

She thought quickly, contrived a shrug which was intended to convey that the matter had little importance.

"You would not call it a reason. I do appreciate your kindness, but I can't let you take such trouble over something which isn't necessary."

"So you are refusing to give me your father's address?"

"I suppose I am, but . . ."

"What are you afraid of?" he demanded in a voice gone cold and deadly. "You *are* afraid of something?"

"No!"

She twisted from the table, too quickly. Her skirt caught the handle of the handbag and sent it to the floor. The contents spilled in a heap, and automatically Felipe was there, scooping up the things and placing them on the polished surface of the table. He straightened, looked down at the silver cigarette case which had escaped from its tissue covering, and took it again into his hand to examine it. For the first time Laurie saw that it was an attractive piece of workmanship with a butterfly-wing inlay and her initial scrolled ornately in one corner.

"I was of the idea that you did not care for smoking," said Felipe.

Through some treacherous trick of human nature she trembled violently. "I . . . I've smoked more lately. You said yourself that . . . that it wouldn't do me any harm to be less serious about my job. I can't get about much, but I can enjoy a cigarette."

"So you bought yourself a pretty case—or someone gave it to you. It does not look quite your taste. You would choose something less flamboyant."

He was armoured in reserve. He snicked the catch open and a snapshot fluttered down and lay face upward on the table. Cedric looked at them, the bland smile of success after the sale of the Tintoretto making him handsome, a fair lock over his brow.

The case was snapped shut and dropped among her modest assortment of possessions. Felipe moved away, and his voice revealed nothing.

"You have doubtless begged Maybury to contact your father; therefore, it is unnecessary for me to do so. It would have been more honest to tell me."

A chill crept over Laurie. She felt a wild impulse to cry out the truth; that she had accepted the cigarette case because it was easier than arguing, that she had never seen it before this moment, when it had slipped from its wrapping, and that the existence of the photograph had surprised her more than it had surprised him.

She must at least make him realize that she had spoken the truth in saying she would be glad when Cedric had gone. He must not believe that there was a bond of any kind between Laurie, her father and Cedric Maybury. But how would he react, taking into consideration the fact that she had withheld the whereabouts of the shop in York?

She was wrenched by a cold and helpless anger against Cedric, who had got what he wanted at her expense. The same could be said of Stella. Because of those two she had to be silent under Felipe's rebuke. The situation was intolerable.

Yet, perhaps, she thought bleakly, this was best. Cedric's cigarette case had accomplished that against which her own protestations had been inadequate. It set the seal upon her reluctance to yield the address Felipe had asked for.

His eyes and mouth were not cruel—as she had seen him before. Both were set in an expression of complete and fastidious withdrawal. He had isolated himself.

He went out to the veranda and looked briefly into the room, but not at Laurie. "I will not say good-bye to the child; he would not comprehend. I have instructed my secretary at the Palacio to make daily enquiries here, and you are to use him if you are in any difficulty before the return of the Senhora Alvares. There is nothing you wish to demand of me?"

So much, that she was near tears. She could not even manage the banality of hoping he would have a pleasant trip.

"Nothing, senhor."

Very well. It is *adeus*."

He bowed and was gone from the range of Laurie's vision. She heard the car start up and purr from the Casa, and long after all sound of him had blown away she still stood there beside the littered table, slumped in misery.

CHAPTER FIFTEEN

SOME DAYS stand out in the memory as bright points of gladness, and others are etched sombrely and unforgettably against a grey background. The day of Felipe's departure was one of the latter kind for Laurie.

At eleven o'clock she knew without a pang that Cedric was starting on his way, but when, at four, she heard a plane and saw it, silver-gilt in the sunshine and heading out over the ocean, her very life seemed to come to an end. Mechanically, she carried on with her duties, and the next day her heart and nerves had settled into a state of numbness.

On the mailship, the one which had taken Cedric, a last letter from Stella had arrived, an epistle so gaily sauve that Laurie had to suppress a dull bitterness. She was instructed to buy new clothes for Richard and to remind the hotel manager that the Alvares' suite, which was never occupied by anyone else, must be opened up and aired for several days, the cocktail cabinet replenished and the Alvares linen and silverware set out as she liked them.

Stella was not the type to turn up unexpectedly. She liked a fanfare; servants palpitating, the red carpet unrolled and a bouquet of the most expensive blossoms to be placed in her arms. Eduardo's affluence assured her of such a welcome wherever she went. In Mondego, where he had no territorial possessions but spent huge sums of money, he was also respected as a close friend of the Marquez. Stella loved her own aura of glory, but was not averse from increasing its lustre by a reflection from Felipe's.

To Sofia's reminder that she had agreed to give a party before leaving the Casa Margarita, Laurie shook her head. Since the *torneios* she had become completely out of tune with the people of Villa Barreiro, and a party at the Casa would cause only awkwardness. They would accept but by their very diffidence create a flop. Mistakenly, they had concluded she was socially above them, and there is no nation more keen than the Portuguese to maintain distinctions between the classes. Sofia must have understood, for she did not protest over much.

To please his mother, Laurie ordered for Richard six new suits from the tailoress who lived in one of the streets which ran up from the Esplanada, in Porto. She also had an unnecessary interview with the hotel manager; that obsequious gentleman had already, of course, received his instructions from Senhor Alvares, and he was mentally rubbing his hands at the prospect of catering for the luncheon and dinner parties which would take place in the Alvares' suite.

Laurie was walking with Richard back to the car which had been parked outside the bank, when she was effusively greeted by a plump matron she vaguely remembered. When the young woman slanted her sunshade and spoke in baby language to Richard, Laurie recalled her name. . . .

"How nice to see you, Senhora Paixas," she said politely. "And how is the little Beatriz," The pudding of a child whom Richard had scorned on the day of the picnic.

It seemed that all was not well with Beatriz; her mother feared she ate too many ice creams and pastries. But few were as fortunate as Senhora Alvares, who could leave her son with Miss Bell and know he would be cared for even better than by a mother. The flowery phrases rolled from Senhora Paixas as if she had memorized them. Beatriz disposed of, she quickly summoned a new topic.

"You must come to see us, Miss Bell. I have a young brother and sister here in Mondego, and they would be very happy to make your acquaintance. They were disappointed not to meet you on the day of the *festa*, at the Palacio. Corina assured us you would be there, and when you were not, she said she would invite us all to an informal dinner at her villa." A lift of the shoulder and the spate continued. "That is off now, of course. You will know that Corina has gone to England. So I will invite you to my house instead. We live in the pink villa at the corner of the Avenida Miguel. . . ."

Senhora Paixas did not finish there, but Laurie heard no more. She felt a dew spring at her temples, plunged a clammy hand into her pocket and with the other took a tighter hold on Richard's fingers.

With the calm of desperation she queried, "Did Senhora Queira travel to England with the Marquez?"

There came a bubbling, embarrassed laugh. "You English! How improper that sounds. Yes, Corina flew with Felipe, but also in the plane were Corina's maid and her aunt, Dona Luize. Felipe, I assure you, displays always the utmost discretion!"

Shortly after that Laurie disentangled herself from the hospitable senhora. Later, when she and Richard sat in the car and were speeding back to Villa Barreiro, she was still shaking, still incapable of clear, connected thinking.

The triumphal return of the Alvares, followed by maids and men-servants and a string of African porters bearing smart grey leather suitcases and trunks upon their backs, was witnessed by Laurie and Richard from the balcony of the private lounge in the Hotel Carnac.

Stella had looked up and waved a white glove. "Hello, my darling! I'm coming straight up."

Before the last of the trunks had been swallowed up by the hotel entrance, Stella was in the lounge and stooping to embrace the mildly astonished Richard.

"Did you miss Mama, my lovely boy? I've got so many presents for you, and Papa has brought you a real live puppy which will be your very own. My sweet, you look good enough to eat!"

Stella did adore the child, Laurie told herself, watching the pale and beautiful face of her sister pressed against the dark brown curls of Richard. The thickset Eduardo, standing above them, had a pleased, famished look, as if he would always be hungry for the love of these two, his wife and his child. Was it because he loved Stella so much that he could bear to be parted from his son, Laurie wondered irrevantly.

Stella was radiant. She threw off a small, clinging hat made of pale grey breast-feathers, pushed delicate fingers through the whitish, silky hair and sparkled at Eduardo. She had apparently been using Portuguese so much that her inflection was almost alien.

"It is like coming home—eh, *querido?*"

He answered her in Portuguese, smiling into her eyes, and in a measure Laurie felt rewarded. It was easy to like Eduardo; one wouldn't willingly hurt him.

"You have been happy, Miss Bell?" he asked presently, when a tea tray had been brought and Stella was pouring. "How was it, living at Villa Barreiro?"

"The Casa Margarita is a pleasant house. Richard had a wonderful time."

"But you," he persisted. "We are very pleased to see that Richard is so well, but I think the heat of Mondego does not suit you."

"We English are often colorless in the heat." said Stella dismissively. "You're quite well, aren't you, Miss Bell?"

"Quite," Laurie answered. She didn't mean to sound ironical; the wry note had crept in, unbidden.

"You see?" Stella told her husband. "It's an English pallor."

"But it is not an English tiredness. Stay and have some tea with us, Miss Bell. We would like to hear of the adventures this *filho* of ours has been having."

Stella approved the invitation with a barely perceptible nod. She smiled down upon Richard's complete engrossment with an array of new plastic toys brought from Lisbon, and held out a cup for Laurie to take.

Laurie told them about the sting-ray and her fright, and Eduardo assured her that he had confidence in her handling of such an incident. Then Richard broke in with a perfect piece of unrehearsed exhibitionism: a number of nursery rhymes strung together and clearly enunciated.

Altogether, it was a pleasanter reunion than Laurie had expected. She had known that Richard had improved, both physically and in the use of his wits, but during the next few days it was Stella who occasionally and accidentally indicated the extent of the improvements.

"How beautifully you manage your spoon, Richard." Or, "How clever of you to make the picture of bricks all by yourself!" And to Laurie she said, "The slight tan suits him so well, doesn't it? And I'm sure he's put on quite a few pounds. It's difficult to believe it's all happened in a couple of months."

Stella, whose only fret had been the frailty of her son, now serenely rode the crest of a wave. Richard bloomed like any other child, and the possessive, maternal pride knew no limits. She hinted that she and Eduardo might give up visiting Mondego, where they had no real interests, and take a house near Lisbon, in which Laurie and Richard could become permanently established. He would need Laurie for several years yet, Stella said reassuringly.

And then what? Laurie did not ask the question because she knew that Stella would promise money as the price of those years. The Senhora Alvares knew no other yard-stick.

Yet one felt that insofar as it was in her to love any man, Stella loved Eduardo, probably because it was through him she had acquired the things for which she had been so frantically ambitious. Before the tour her feelings where her husband was concerned had been less apparent; they had seemed to be a compound of respect, the purring quality of being loved for one's beauty, and the merest hint of gratitude. But during her absence from Mondego a subtle change had come over Stella, and it was symptomatic of it that she should make an allusion to something of the sort when she happened to be alone on the balcony with Laurie one evening, after Richard was in bed.

The sky had an indigo warmth and the stars hung low. The usual guitarist was strolling along the esplanade and the song he sang praised a certain senhorita whose hair was like the raven and whose eyes were diamond-bright. The cicadas scraped their wings ecstatically, and a breeze stirred the scented air.

"The evenings are marvellous," said Laurie pensively.

"Any night here is a night for lovers," commented Stella in her measured, polished tones. "It's like this in the summer in Portugal. You can't wonder at the young men and women being terribly aware of one another; it's an urgent, physical awareness. There's something in the atmosphere which makes romantic love assume more importance than it really deserves."

"Perhaps you have to be Portuguese—or married to one—to feel it," said Laurie.

"Meaning, I suppose, that you're too bedrock to notice it. I'm pretty objective about that kind of thing myself, but I wouldn't confess as much to a man. Men of all ages like to feel they can inspire romance in a woman, but after marriage most women allow their children to get in the way."

"The art of marriage is said to be a fusion of mother love with the love romantic." Laurie looked at her sister curiously. "I believe you're learning the art, Stella."

The china blue eyes sharpened swiftly. "Don't ever make the error of using my christian name in front of others, will you? I don't find it difficult to call you Miss Bell, because I make a practice of thinking of you continually in those terms."

"How sweet," said Laurie drily. "I'll try always to think of you as Senhora Alvares."

Stella had the grace to raise an apologetic hand. "I'm sorry about it, but it hasn't really affected you, has it? You do realize it's the only way?"

"Of course."

"You don't think me ungratefull?"

"Why should I? You pay me a good salary and you're entitled to make the conditions."

Stella did something unusual for her; she hesitated, as if not too certain how to frame what she intended to convey. "Eduardo likes you, and he's very anxious that we should do everything to make you happy. He says you have a lost look."

Laurie hardened against a threatened invasion of her privacy. "You should know me better than he does."

"I told him that as you haven't any knowledge of Portuguese you've probably been a little lonely, but that it would be better for you now that we're back. You must be with us more—have a meal with us sometimes, and perhaps even go to the Casino. I hear that you've had invitations from some of our friends, so they won't regard it as strange if we take you with us occasionally."

To Laurie's own surprise she was not hurt. Perhaps the bitterness in her was too acute to be affected by those recurring pinpricks dealt by Stella. She looked at her sister dispassionately, saw the pure, elegant profile, emeralds drooping in a platinum setting from a small ear, and white shoulders rising from a gown of rich figured brocade. It was extraordinary how one so sophisticated could remain oblivious to her effect on other women; knowing herself beautiful, she just didn't care what they thought.

Stella had never suffered. She had worried over Richard's chills and lack of strength, but her security had never really been tilted; and now, with Eduardo deeper in love with her than ever and the child gaining health, she was even more entrenched in the world she had chosen.

No, the harshness in Laurie's throat was not from pain through Stella's thoughtless condescension. It came from the ache of yearning and desolation which was never completely absent these days.

The guitarist had wandered too far away for his next song to be dissected, but if one waited long enough another serenader would turn up; they always did, drawn down to the sea by a nameless enchantment. Out there, Indians were drifting by in couples and groups, the women in shimmering saris and the men wearing European suits. There was doubtless a festival at the temple and these people had come in from their small plantations to enjoy it. The climate of Mondego seemed conducive to feasting and dancing; to making merry and making love.

Stella tossed her cigarette over the parapet. "I haven't really thanked you for all you're doing for Richard," she said. "I do appreciate it—very much. It was wonderful to be able to go away knowing that he couldn't possibly be in better hands. I didn't worry about him at all. Believe it or not," Stella gave that low yet tinkling laugh, "the tour was like a second honeymoon; better, in fact, because I'm not so raw as I was then. It was a great idea of mine, to get you out here to look after him!"

Fortunately, Eduardo came from the bedroom just then, and Stella turned back into the room. Laurie heard him softly pay her a compliment in Portuguese.

Then Stella said clearly, "I've been telling Miss Bell that she must go with us to the Casino one evening."

"That is so," he promptly concurred, with a kindly smiling glance at Laurie as he came from the balcony.

"You are needing some life, Miss Bell! We will arrange it for tomorrow."

Laurie thanked him and went to her own room. The face which looked back at her from her mirror was white and forlorn, but she resolutely touched it up and went down to her table for one in the hotel dining-room.

Each night she went to bed worn out, yet her brain refused to give in till nearly dawn. She awakened unrefreshed, loaded down by a sensation of imminent disaster which took hours to wear off. Her father had often said that if one turned one's back upon trouble it grew to tremendous proportions, that only by facing and analyzing it could one arrive at a cure.

But was there a cure for the kind of love which soaks into one's being and leaves no room for anything else? After days and nights of wrenching conjecture, Laurie concluded that no remedy existed in Mondego.

Because Eduardo would have been distressed had she refused, she accompanied him and Stella and several of their friends to the Casino. It was not a den of insensate gambling. At the cocktail hour a small orchestra played on the terrace, and after dinner the tables were fairly crowded, though few played above the minimum stake of fifteen escudos. Only tourists gambled specifically to win.

Another evening, at the invitation of one of Eduardo's friends, she danced in the hotel ballroom, a magnificent place which had one end open to the tropical night. After dancing she had wandered with the crowd into the garden for a drink at one of the long tables under the trees, and there they had all sat, airing local gossip. It was Stella who had mentioned Felipe's visit to England.

"How appalling," she had said to her attentive friends, "if he decided to stay in England for several months. Even worse, if he decided to marry there!"

"My dear," said a thin woman in a silver lace mantilla, "Felipe would never act with so little consideration for us. Always he does everything with the utmost propriety, and he has not even announced his engagement to Corina Queira."

Here, the plump young Senhora Paixas leaned forward, knowledgeably nodding her head so that her ear-rings sparkled. "But there is something between those two, I assure you. Corina promised that we should know, but she went away before we had an opportunity to learn more. There is an arrangement of some kind, you may be certain, or she would not have travelled with him. Such a pity, Stella, that you were not here. You and Eduardo are his close friends; he would have told you his plans."

Stella smiled graciously, accepting the compliment. "If he is to prolong his stay in England, you may take it that he will let us know. Don't you think so, Eduardo?"

Her husband bent across the table, and Laurie's nerves tightened till she thought the tension must be plain for all to see in her features. Eduardo was honest and sane; she had the fatal conviction that he would expose the truth of the matter. Be compassionate, Eduardo, she pleaded silently.

"I think," he said, twinkling, "that my wife will be a little jealous when Felipe marries. He has often declared that if there were another Stella in the world he would make her his wife. Me, I think he is resigned to there being only one Stella." Laurie relaxed slightly, only to curl her fingers back into her palms at his next words. "We people who are old friends of Felipe and think we know him have foolishly prepared ourselves for the unexpected; but he himself has confounded us by escorting the Senhora Queira to England. She is, after all, the daughter of the Conde de Garda."

A strange compulsion made Laurie say, "I don't believe the Marquez attached much importance to the fact that Senhora Queira and her aunt were accompanying him in the plane."

Stella stared at her with more than a hint of hateur, and said coolly, "What can you know about it, Miss Bell?"

There was a brief, awkward silence. Laurie, brought up sharp by the reminder that though she was now permitted within the Alvares' social circle, she was still an employee of the senhora, had to take a minute or two to readjust her thoughts, and before she could answer, the eager Senhora Paixas had stepped in.

"Have you not heard of the little adventure shared by Felipe and your admirable Miss Bell, Stella? It was at the finals of the *torneios* at Villa Barreiro. . . ." The voluble woman gave an extravagant description of Almeido's wound and the subsequent dressing of it in the performers' marquee. "My brother was there in the tent," she finished. "He told me he would have given much to be either Almeido or Felipe!"

Bright coins of color sprang into Laurie's pale cheeks; they were unmistakable in the glow from the lamp which hung from a branch above the table. "It was nothing at all," she said stiffly. "The Marquez could have managed without me."

"Our Miss Bell," said Eduardo paternally, "is modest. She is one of your people who prefer to do good by stealth."

And there it was left for the present. Attention turned to the horse-racing which would take place in about a fortnight, to the formation of a polo club which might also play matches on the mainland, and to the chances of good rock-fishing in the near future. There was more dancing, and a walk along the promenade before these people, who were accustomed to late hours, dispersed to their beds.

CHAPTER SIXTEEN

DURING THE following day Laurie became aware more than once of Stella's cold and calculating glance, but just what that clear regulated brain was working upon she could only guess. She spent most of the time with Richard, took him to a small private zoo, and afterwards drew outlines of the animals for him to color.

She dined in her room that evening, and as it was Anita's night off she went back to the suite and sat in the lounge, reading. Noises came up from the esplanade, the slamming of car doors, a blur of dance music which somehow had an eastern rhythm in keeping with Mondego's position in the Indian Ocean.

It must have been nearly eleven when Stella came in, alone. She paused inside the room, then swiftly and decisively turned the key in the lock. Laurie was looking her way but did not stir.

With a natural, feline grace, Stella came to the centre of the room and dropped her mink stole upon the table. She raised an arm glistening with jewels, smoothed the silver-blonde hair at her temple and, characteristically, stroked a finger along the graceful line of her jaw.

"I came up to get a lighter wrap," she said.

Laurie waited. She knew the wrap was merely an excuse to cover the genuine reason. People fell over themselves to fetch and carry for Stella.

"I also came," her sister added, "because I knew you were here alone, and I wanted a word with you."

It was late, and Laurie was too mentally fatigued besides to brace herself. She sensed what was coming and hardly cared.

"Go ahead," she said briefly.

"First," Stella was using those carefully crisp tones which were devoid of all feeling, "I'm afraid I have to warn you to be more discreet when you happen to be among our friends. I can't have you butting in when we talk about such a man as Felipe de Velho Barreiro."

Laurie said steadily, "I hate to have caused you a second's uneasiness. In fact, I don't believe I did. You're simply reminding me of the threat you made before you went away. But you needn't. I remember every word."

"You're calm, aren't you?" Stella's scarlet lips compressed into a line. "Now that Eduardo has shown his gratitude for the way you've cared for Richard you feel secure. Perhaps you even have it in mind that one day he'll get to know exactly who you are. If so, let me correct those thoughts, here and now!"

Laurie laid aside her book and stood up. "You haven't much faith in others, have you, Stella? I beg your pardon—senhora. Aren't you in the least curious to know how much you really mean to Eduardo? In your shoes I'd have to confess and find out."

Stella broke in with a laugh which was both edged and contemptuous. "You could never be in my shoes. You haven't got what it takes to snaffle a rich husband, let alone keep him in love with you. I don't want your girlish advice, Laurie." Her manner altered. "I'm not quarreling with you, but these things have to be said."

"For your peace of mind," nodded Laurie, wearily comprehending.

"Exactly. I've told you before that I won't have you trying to make friends with Felipe, and I also warned you not to become seriously friendly with any of the men here. I took it that you'd have the sense to see how utterly foolish it would be. What does this Almeido Gourros mean to you?"

"Not a thing."

"Is that the truth?" Laurie looked her answer, and Stella added quickly, "All right, I believe you. Will you also give me your word that you haven't formed a real attachment for any man in Mondego?"

"No," said Laurie without a tremor, "I won't. It isn't your business, Stella."

Stella's thin nostrils dilated and her eyes were sapphire hard, yet there was very little change in her voice. "You're becoming daring. I wonder why? Is it because you've fallen so hard for someone that Father and Richard don't matter any more? If it is. . . ."

Laurie shook her head. "Don't worry. I'll always safeguard Daddy's quarterly cheque—which means that your secret is as secure as it ever was."

But even as she spoke she was uncertain. Stella might insist on her remaining in Mondego for much longer than she could bear it. And now, at this moment, she felt like getting out and running away, jumping a boat which would take her anywhere, away from the island. It was a most stupid way to feel, of course, because Stella wouldn't have that, either. Laurie Bell was bound to Senhora Alvares for as long as she was needed.

Her reflections, culminating in hopelessness, must have been very apparent, for Stella, after appraising her critically, drew a brief, satisfied sigh and said approvingly, "That's fine. We really understand each other awfully well. You will bear in mind the necessity for discretion when you happen to be with our friends, won't you? Oh, and by the way, I've a length of pink organdie which would make you a pretty evening frock. Pink suits you golden-brown people. I had you in mind when I bought it, in Oporto."

Stella's smile was the bright, uncomplicated one of victory. She went into the bedroom and came out carrying a shoulder cape of white ring velvet lined with lilac silk that matched the suit she was wearing. When she had gone, the mink stole still lay where she had carelessly thrown it on the table, giving off its costly, elusive perfume.

Laurie sank into her chair and crossed her arms behind her head. She thought back to the day in England when she had received Stella's letter, inviting her to Mondego. She hadn't realized then that her sister's proposition was a trap, and she'd been prepared to forget the less pleasant aspects of Stella's character as she had known it in childhood.

Henry Fielding had been quietly joyful. He had always found Stella's selfishness easy to forgive, because she was his daughter and very lovely. He cherished the notion that as people grow older they cannot help but acquire wisdom, and Stella, he had contended, must inevitably have mellowed with marriage and motherhood. They were the softening influences she had needed.

How wrong both he and Laurie had been. Here was Stella, queening it over her husband and his friends, unshakably established by her beauty, poise and riches. She had wanted the best for herself and gone all out to capture it. Later, she had demanded the best for her son, and taken steps to secure that, too. To Stella, there had never been any real danger in having Laurie near, because not only did she trust her young sister but her faith in her own ability to handle others was founded on her bank balance. Laurie, she had probably suspected, was not to be bought; but she had correctly assessed the relationship between Henry Fielding and his younger daughter, and profited thereby.

Laurie stared up at the carved panelling of the ceiling: Indian oak with white insets and a scroll at every intersection. She recalled some of the murals and ceiling paintings she had seen in Mondego, and like an arrow to its target her thoughts went straight to the wealth of artistic treasures at the Palacio.

Felipe had been gone for three weeks. Where was he now? In London, meeting old friends and introducing Corina as the future Marquez? Corina's dark good looks and attractively accented English would go down well in England, and there, among people who were so different, she would have an even stronger appeal for Felipe, who, in spite of his English blood in outlook was almost wholly Portuguese.

Perhaps he had taken her there deliberately, with the object of seeing her in the country house which had belonged for generations to his mother's people; Corina against the background which had been the old Marqueza's. At this time of the year it would be cold and damp in the Cotswolds, and to him Corina would have all the warmth and color of Portugal and Mondego. Perhaps he wished her to decide about selling the estate. Only Felipe's wife would have the power to alter decisions made by his mother.

For a moment Laurie permitted herself the bitter luxury of visualizing herself in other circumstances; but only for a moment. It was unlikely that Laurie Fielding could have found a way into Felipe's heart, but Miss Bell was now and for ever outside it.

Was it right to regard herself as irrevocably linked up with Stella's schemes? Wasn't it possible that now her father could purchase an occasional genuine antique the shop was making more money? Not that there was a tremendous sale for antiques in York, and this was the lean season. She wouldn't be able to act before spring, and by then. . . .

Normally, but tonight the doors wide open to the balcony awakened poignant memories. Of Felipe, of course, The breeze breathed his name, and she saw him that first day, at lunch time, when he had come in with the sun slanting across his thick dark hair and a faintly sardonic smile on the finely-cut lips; knowing her, but deliberately not knowing her.

She had seen him in other moods since then; the urbane host, the inimitable friend, the mocking companion, the angry benefactor, and all of them—yes, even his anger—had in the ultimate filled her with a dumb, aching tenderness. It seemed impossible that the few past weeks could have held so much transient pleasure and lasting pain, so much false hope and imagining.

Not that she had wallowed in the improbable—in fact, she had shown remarkable private restraint—but hope is ever a constituent of love, and dimly she had had the wild conviction that in pite of Felipe's position, in spite of seeming impossibilities, she could have been the smiling, adoring wife he needed.

In about a week he would be back in Mondego, though perhaps not for long. Now that she and Richard had left Villa Barreiro, and Stella was on hand to relieve him of his duty to his godson, he would come to the Carnac only as an occasional visitor. In her bones Laurie knew that her own problematical friendship with Felipe de Velho Barreiro was ended, and her duty to her own self-respect was to look for something to take its place.

One night, with as much chance of success, seek to obliterate the spots of the leopard.

Laurie did not remind Stella of the promised gift of pink organdie. She wanted nothing from her sister but the salary which she was carefully hoarding against the future. It appeared, though, that Eduardo's conscience was more vulnerable than his wife's. He was continually delighted with Richard's swift progress from a puny, lifeless baby into an increasingly robust little boy, and felt that no reward for Laurie was too great.

It was on the Firday of that week that he bought her a wrist-watch. Just before noon Laurie dragged Richard's gocart into the vestibule of the hotel. An attendant hurried forward to relieve her and she saw Eduardo standing at a wine table, on the other side of which lounged his languidly-graceful wife. As usual after a couple of hours amusing the child on the beach, Laurie was sticky and tired, but as Eduardo came towards her she gave him a dutiful smile and lifted Richard from the cart.

Eduardo's dark face creased into an answering smile. "You are indefatigable, Miss Bell. Come and have a refresher with us."

"Richard should go to bed for an hour. We're already a little late, senhor."

"But your methods are commonsense and elastic," he said. "You do not scrub the child wide awake before putting him to rest. Come, a quick drink."

When they reached Stella, her blue glance rested exclusively upon Richard. "Well, my pretty boy. Tell Mama what you have been doing.

"He is tired, my dear," said Eduardo. "What will you drink, Miss Bell? I suggest passion fruit juice with an enlivening dash of gin. Yes?"

The drinks were brought. Richard stood lolling against Laurie but staring, sleepy-eyed, at the fair and wonderful creature who was his mother. Laurie often suspected that in the tales she told him the fairy queen had for him the remote, aquiline loveliness of Stella.

So unobtrusively that Laurie was taken by surprise, Eduardo opened a small, long case and placed it in front of her on the low table.

"The senhora and I chose this for you today," he said. "We hope you will accept it as a very small token of our regard for you."

"Why . . . why, thank you, senhor."

The watch was tiny, square and gold on a thin bracelet of gold and platinum. It made the one on her wrist, given to her by her father three years ago when she had badly needed it, look cheap and clumsy.

Stella drawled softly, "The idea was my husband's. He had bought some diamonds for me in Lisbon which the jeweller here—who is an excellent craftsman—is setting into a necklace. We called to see how it was going." A pause, during which, Laurie supposed, she was intended to weigh up the vast difference between a gold wrist-watch, however costly, and a diamond necklace built up from specially selected gems. Then Stella murmured to Richard, "And how is that comical puppy? Don't you like him?"

"He bites," came the answer on a happy sigh. "Woofie doesn't bite."

On the gentle wave of laughter following this, Laurie escaped; but not before Eduardo had said, "Have lunch at our table today, Miss Bell. At one-fifteen."

Upstairs, Laurie quickly dabbed most of the grubbiness from Richard's face and hands and helped him to leap the cot-rails. When he was settled she went to her own room for a bath and to change into something suitable for luncheon with Senhor and Senhora Alvares.

She chose a green and white striped silk with a nipped-in waist and wide neckline, brushed her hair into the rough, yellow-brown curls which made her face small and fine in comparison. She fastened the new watch about her wrist, and knew the sensation which is every woman's when she wears something expensive and very simple. She would still use the other watch, though, and keep this one for the best. And she would always regard it as a gift from Eduardo, not from Stella. That way she would enjoy wearing it.

After ordering Richard's lunch and instructing Anita, she went downstairs and through the vestibule to the smaller lounge. Eduardo and Stella had already had an apéritif, and when Laurie had declined one, all three moved through to the dining room.

Unaccountably, that luncheon had a faintly gala atmosphere. Stella, in ivory silk with touches of sea-blue, a deep collaret of exquisitely-graded pearls about her throat, showed an almost insolent enjoyment of the wines and delicacies served by the waiter who attended no other table but this. Eduardo was in good form, exhibiting his conventional but Latin sense of humor, and Laurie found herself reflecting that perhaps in Portugal, far from all these people with whom she had become acquainted, life with Richard and his parents might be tolerable, even if it could never be satisfying.

They had coffee in a secluded corner of the terrace which looked out over lawns and palms but gave a view, in one direction, of the hotel entrance and the courtyard. Laurie smoked a cigarette with them, squashed out the butt and dusted ash from her dress.

"I think I'd better go and see what's happening to Richard," she said.

Stella wasn't listening. She was leaning to one side, to get a better sight of the courtyard. "There's Felipe!" she exclaimed. "Did you know he had arrived, Eduardo?"

Laurie whitened, but did not turn round. She heard Eduardo say, "He was not back early this morning. I spoke to his secretary and he told me he had no news."

But apparently there was no need for this. Felipe came striding down the terrace with his usual lithe grace. In the white drill he looked very tall and very dark; he looked something else, too, which Laurie's glance at him was too hasty to define, though she saw it. She got quickly to her feet and found him close.

"You have been unwell, senhorita?" he demanded at once, with brusque concern.

Laurie contrived a little smile. "No, senhor."

Stella extended a white hand. As Felipe bent over it her hard blue eyes sent out to Laurie a shaft of warning and dismissal, but her voice was honey-smooth. "We've missed you, Felipe. We thought you were not due back till next Wednesday."

"My business was finished, so I came," he said, abruptly for him. "The plane took four interminable days for the trip."

"How, then," enquired Eduardo. "Are you so anxious to be here in Mondego? Was England grim?"

"England was not grim." Felipe glanced swiftly from one to the other of them and asked perfunctorily, "You had a good tour, you two?"

"It was perfect," said Stella. "Sit down, Felipe. Have you had lunch?"

He snapped his fingers impatiently, as if he might be on the edge of violence. "What I have to say is more important than lunch."

Stella's interest was patent in her smile. "But surely you can sit down to say it, Felipe. I don't believe I've ever seen you so . . . so taut. What can possibly have happened to make you like that?"

Now, Laurie forced herself to look at him properly. The dark eyes were glittering, yet he appeared tired and unhappy. Felipe . . . unhappy. Her heart moved with love and fright. Something terrible must have befallen Corina.

"I'll go," she said in a voice not much above a whisper.

"You will stay," he said curtly. "What I have to say concerns all of us, and I will not have you running away."

Her knees were trembling so much that she was thankful to sit down again. Felipe lowered himself to the fourth chair, and that tautness of his pervaded the whole of that corner of the terrace. Stella sat immobile, watching. Eduardo's set smile was interrogative but very slightly uneasy. Laurie was dazed and quivering, and trying hard to concentrate on the beaten metal ashtray in front of her, though she really saw nothing but Felipe's fingers clenched into a ruthless fist on the edge of the table.

CHAPTER SEVENTEEN

EDUARDO BROUGHT that ghastly silence to an end. "Felipe, my friend, you have us all intrigued."

Felipe gave one of those smiles which leave the eyes hard and purposeful. He stared straight at Eduardo, ignoring both women—which in itself was an indication of the extra-ordinary state of his emotions. "You are going to dislike me for this, but that cannot be helped. Friendship does survive cruel blows and so will ours, I think." His pause just then was more potent than his statement. Then he added, "Eduardo, did you know that your wife and this child here are sisters?"

Eduardo's expression went absolutely blank. Obviously, in face of such a question he found it difficult to think, and quite impossible to give an answer. Stella, to her credit, scarcely fluttered a muscle, but she lost color and sat very still.

Oddly, it was Laurie who stepped into the chasm. "Where on earth did you hear that?" she asked unsteadily. "The queerest rumours get about."

Felipe's tone placed a wall between them. "Do not intensify the wrongness with lies," he said tersely. And to Eduardo: "Stella must forgive me for the straight speaking. I am determined to put the matter right. You were not aware of this, were you, *amigo*?"

Eduardo spoke as if his lips were stiff. "I . . . was not. Nor can I quite believe it. Stella has no sister, she has no one." But as he turned to his wife the conviction was gone from his manner and his tone was low. "Felipe is mistaken, is he not, my dear?"

It may have been kindness to Stella or intolerance of the whole situation which made Felipe continue to ignore her.

"I am not mistaken," he said. "I have learned all this at first hand, in England. Your Miss Bell is Laurie Fielding, sister to Stella. They have a nice old father who owns a quaint shop full of treasures in one of the streets of York; I have seen the shop." He leaned over the table and in spite of his determination to hurt Eduardo as little as possible, his teeth snapped. "I have also spoken with Henry Fielding, who is, as Laurie has once told me, sweet and unpractical and wholly likeable. You would not be ashamed to own him as a father-in-law, Eduardo!"

Stella was intent upon the fingers locked tightly together in her lap. Eduardo had averted himself from her, but he said: "You do not do me justice, Felipe. I would never be ashamed of Stella's relatives, whoever they might be." He passed a hand across his forehead. "You must pardon me if I seem dull, but I cannot understand this. You, Miss Bell," his bewilderment was tinged with pain as he corrected himself, "Laurie . . . is it true that you and Stella have connived to deceive every one? You have allowed me to treat you as a servant, even to reprimand you for omitting to call your . . . your sister senhora. . . ."

For a minute it seemed as if the whole thing were too devastating for Eduardo; possibly he was remembering the imperiousness with which Stella had treated her sister and his own pardonable condescension. Laurie could see, as the men could not, that the humiliation had bitten too deeply into Stella for her yet to be capable of words; that Felipe of all men should find this out and state it so irrefutably! She felt suddenly terribly sorry for both of them, and angry with Felipe.

"You've always been kind to me, Eduardo," she said quickly, warmly, "and even if you'd known all about me it wouldn't have made any difference. I'd have looked after Richard while you were away, just the same." Her breath came unevenly. "It's been so good, to know all the time that he was my nephew. That was why Stella asked me to come here, you know. She explained it all to me at the beginning, and I . . . she swallowed on the untruth, "I didn't mind."

"But you had arranged never to tell me," said Eduardo.

"I think we might have told you, some time. You see. . . ."

"White lies," cut in Felipe with icy politness, "are nearly as reprehensible as black ones. The fact is, Eduardo, that Stella was afraid to acknowledge this dear man who buys and sells as her father; she feared that so mundane a background would detract from her charms. Having decided, when you first met, that she loved you enough to marry you, she also decided to cut herself off from the father and the sister."

"She didn't really cut herself off," Laurie put in on Stella's behalf. "She wrote to us and we loved hearing about you and Richard."

Eduardo drew his lip between his teeth. He and Stella were still unable to meet each other's eyes, and Laurie, in the midst of her anxiety, could not help but admire the calm with which both strove to meet calamity. Deep inside she had wanted Eduardo to learn the truth about Stella, but this was not the method she herself would have chosen. How much better if Stella had forced herself to confess when they were alone.

She felt Felipe watching her, and she returned his regard as frigidly as she could. How dare he go to York after she had refused to give him her father's address! And how beastly to expose Stella like this. What could have come over him to compel him to such action—he, in whom chivalry was inbred? And he called himself Stella's friend!

Possibly he divined what Laurie was thinking, for he said steadily. "It is my belief, Eduardo, that your wife has regretted for a long time the impulse which made her deny the existence of her family. Your feelings about this are trifling compared with hers; it *was* merely an impulse, for which she is now paying. My dear Stella," he was as courteous and charming as ever, "you are pained now, but presently I think you will be very relieved. Eduardo loves you too much to permit this little discovery to mar your marriage, and you will have the happiness of teaching your son that he has a grandfather—one whom he will love with all his heart. We are all foolish at times."

"All of us except Felipe," said Laurie bitterly.

"Even I!" he exclaimed sharply.

Stella raised her head. The blue eyes were cold and empty. "I haven't a thing to say."

"*Minha cara,*" began Eduardo, distressed.

But Laurie sprang to her feet. All the malaise and numbness were gone. She wanted to bruise Felipe as he had bruised Eduardo and Stella; and perhaps she also felt a need to stab him for all the anguish and hopelessness which were corroding her own heart.

"Why did you have to seek out my father? You knew it was against my will yet you did it, deliberately. Even before Stella went away you mentioned that you noticed a likeness between us, and gradually you suspected the truth, didn't you? How amusing you must have found it! What immense pleasure it must have given you to go ferreting out a secret which hurt nobody and might eventually have come to light naturally, without causing so much unhappiness. If you wanted to get back at me for that horrible picture you bought, you've done it!"

Three of them were standing now; Stella still sat like a statue, staring upwards, though a faint, astonished alarm showed in her marble features.

Felipe's eyes were narrow, his mouth tight. "This had no connection with the picture," he said rapidly. "I trusted you and suspected nothing. I would not say there is a strong likeness between you and Stella, even now that I know. Once I had learned the truth this had to be made right. I detest injustice, whoever the victim."

"I'm not a child or a waif." Laurie was trembling again, much more violently than before. "You've just about spoiled everything, with your beastly sense of justice—which I'd rather call vindictiveness!"

Felipe towered, hot with rage. "I will not have you speak to me like that! There is nothing in this situation which will not be the better for honesty between us. You are entitled to the use of your own name, and to be known as Stella's sister."

"Felipe is right, Laurie." Stella had made the effort to get to her feet. The reddened lips were stark in the pallor of her face, but she had obviously utilized the breathing space while others argued to line up the facts to the best advantage. "Our little plan was silly; it was bound to come to pieces some time and cause an upset like this. We meant well, but the longer we postponed being frank with Eduardo the more gruelling it would have been. I'm glad he knows. I can even find it in my heart to be grateful to Felipe, and sorry that we've made him angry."

Laurie recognized the brief speech for what it was: a bid for the men's sympathy. But she was too keyed up to play up any longer to Stella. She flashed round upon Filipe, her throat working.

"Now that you've put the Fielding family where they belong, I hope you're satisfied; You've lived up to your code, and that's all that matters. I don't think I've ever hated anyone so much in my life."

She turned and fled blindly along the terrace. Her first intention was to get to her room and lock herself in. Then the very thought of being closed in while everything was so incoherent was not to be borne. She wanted to lie down in the grass somewhere and weep till she was exhausted.

But a hand slid about her arm and gripped. "We will take a little walk," said a clipped, savage voice. "You will continue this interesting discussion with the man you hate. Come with me!"

A verbal refusal could have made no difference, for that hand, electrified with an almost brute strength, compelled her to go wh re he willed.

To the consterna..on of the hotel servants who knew this to be the hours for siesta, the Marquez and his companion went quickly down the terrace steps into a long garden shaded by palms, and disappeared into a neat shrubbery.

Felipe was brought up sharply by an ornamental wall overhung by acacias. Quite roughly, he took her shoulder and made her face him, but his eyes were so hot and brilliant with anger that she turned her head.

Her words tumbled as if she hardly knew what she was saying. "I shouldn't have exploded like that, but you don't know how it is—you can't realize how I feel about it. It's not for myself, or for Stella. My father's always been so proud of Stella . . . and there was the money she sent him . . . she needn't have sent it, but she did. It was through me that you found out. It will be my fault if Stella and Eduardo are estranged, and you'll never understand. . . ."

"Be quiet and let me talk. You have already said far too much! Eduardo and Stella will not be estranged. She is too clever, that sister of yours, to lose a man who adores her. Always it has been that she must have everything and now she must suffer a little, which will perhaps improve that stony nature of hers."

Laurie glanced fleetingly at those eyes which glittered topaz in the strong daylight. "Weren't you . . . taken in by her?"

"No, my dear Laurie," he said swiftly, sarcastically, "I was not taken in. I would have to be in love with her before my imagination would paint a soul in those starry blue eyes, and I can assure you, I am not that! She makes Eduardo happy, and for me that is enough. Now, about this father of yours—he is still proud of Stella, and of you, also."

"You mean . . ."

"I mean that he has guessed nothing. It was his tenderness for you both that made him tell me so much. He was delighted by my visit."

"Oh." She leaned against the wall, rested her elbow upon it and pressed the hand to her eyes. Weakly, she said, "I expect you think I'm mad."

"Not mad," he answered curtly. "You are impulsive and ungrateful. You have too much independence and insufficient trust, and I am beginning to ask myself if you are any more able to love than is your sister. But you are not mad."

"I'm sorry I said what I did—back there."

"So you are sorry," he said, in a curiously dry, flat voice. "That is fine. It excuses everything. I am one to be hated, one who is vindictive, but you are sorry, and now all is put right." His nostirls were thinned and white, but the control was still there, rigid in his tones. "It does not interest you why I was so anxious to see your father?"

There came the sudden tiny scream of an insect in the branches above. Laurie' nerves, already raw, seemed to screech an answer, and her hand clenched whitely on the stone wall.

"Was it . . . Cedric?"

"*Por deus,* it was not that creature!" He drew a sharp breath. "I went to see your father because I was impelled by my own emotions. I told him that I had a great affection for you—that with his permission I would one day—when you had grown to love me enough—ask you to be my wife."

Laurie swayed back for the complete support of the wall. Scarlet petals flowered in her cheeks and the grey eyes filled with fright and incredulity. Had her whole future depended on it she could not have spoken. She could only hang on to the wall and stare.

A muscle jerked in his jaw. "Unbelievable, is it not? But we Portuguese are incomprehensible people — so opposed in ways to the British. We fall in love, we are furiously jealous! And some of us are stupid enough to wish to light fires where they cannot exist!"

It was too much for Laurie, a heady wine with a stinging bitterness in every sip. "Your wife- Marry you?" she breathed. "You . . . you're worked up. You can't know what you've just said."

"I am saying what I would have said two months ago, if there had been no cheap art dealer peddling imitations! You are still yearning for that cheat."

"Indeed I'm not!" The blood which had begun to pound in her veins gave strength to her voice. She looked up at him, her eyes gone misty and sweet. "Felipe—please say it again—that you want me to love you."

His face, as he bent over her, was dark and unsmiling. His mouth scarcely moved. " You must love me, Laurita," he said indistinctly. " You must love me with every part of your mind and with every fraction of a heartbeat. Because that is how I love you, how I shall always love you."

"Oh, darling," she whispered, and a tear spilled down her cheek.

He took her fiercely into his arms. His chin pressed against her temple, and his speech became even thicker. He talked of love; there was magic in his touch as he stroked her hair, and bliss, unmeasured bliss in the unending pressure of his mouth upon her own. She felt she was swooning, the conscious world had slipped away and only their own presence existed; a heaven that Laurie had never even dreamed about—and it was here!

Yet when at last he took her shoulders and held her away from him, a tremendous shyness had possession of her. Not to Felipe, however.

"You feel as I do?" he demanded urgently. "Just a little?"

"A whole lot," she told him shakily. "How did it come about, Felipe? How could you possibly fall in love with me?"

"It was like slipping over the edge of a waterfall. It happened—I cannot say when it happened. Perhaps a minute after we met, when you defied me. That morning, down on the coast road. . . ." He snapped his fingers, remembering. "You had seen Stella, had you not?" She had made you agree to her proposition and you were annoyed and distressed?"

She nodded. "And to me you seemed so very much of Stella's world—which I considered artificial and horrid—that I disliked you at sight."

"You have been disliking me, now and again, ever since!" As if to punish her he kissed her once more, with painful ardour, and in due course went on gravely, "That deception was a wicked thing—to you and to me. You should never have concurred."

"I was tied." Her heart was so full, her happiness so tremulously whole, that she was beginning to pity Stella. "I loathe it, but I couldn't help realizing Stella's predicament."

"So you acquiesced, in order that your sister's charity to your father should not cease. That is what it was—charity! I have told you that you have too much pride, my dear heart, too much independence, but it is right that every one should be proud in some degree. Your father shall have his pride and independence. I will see to it myself."

"Felipe, you're so good."

He laughed on a note of strain. "I did not feel that I would be good to you when I arrived back today. For days my mind has been disordered about this business. What would occur, I have enquired of myself, if I had not recollected that your father's shop was called 'Miscellany,? I would have searched for someone named Bell who had a daughter in Mondego, and I would not have met him. Also, if you were to find that you loved me, you would not even to yourself admit it. Too much has depended on the small incident when I admired your pomander box and you told me something of your home." He smote the stone wall. "Those were the thoughts which haunted me! When I came upon you there on the terrace looking so pale and beautiful, and so ready to carry on with this foolish masquerade, I could have taken you with these two hands and hurt you very much."

She gazed at him in love and wonder. A hot wind moved the trees and a thin foam of yellow wafted down from the acacia flowers. A bird muttered crossly to companions who were doubtless crowding his branch, and the cicadas went on sleepily chirring. At this hour the heat was palpable and overpowering.

"We must find somewhere for you to rest," Felipe said. "Not your room, because I must stay near and talk to you."

"I ought to go to Richard."

"You are no longer his nurse. If I am not mistaken, Stella and Eduardo have already gone to their suite; they will look after their own child, and besides have much to discuss. You will find—after you are married!—that siesta is a time for confidences between husband and wife." He slid an arm across her shoulders and added teasingly, "The blush is becoming. I intend to cause it very often. Come, *amorsinha,* we will take possession of a garden shelter!"

In vain she protested she was not tired. He made her lie in the long canvas seat inside a stone shelter which was open to the sea, and sat himself facing her in a grass chair. For minutes they were content merely to look at each other with a half-smile of ecstatic discovery.

Then Laurie said, "Poor Stella. I wish you'd taxed her with it privately, Felipe."

"No," he said decisively, "It was too bad for that. It will do her good to be less sure of herself, to have to trouble in a different way to keep Eduardo's affection."

"I believe she really loves him quite deeply."

"My dearest, you believe the best of every one—even of Stella. She is not in love with him because she could never love anyone but Stella, but she does derive boundless pleasure from being loved by him. The French have a saying that there is always one who loves and one who allows himself to be loved. That is Eduardo and your sister."

"It's not us," she said softly.

"We could not bear that, either of us."

"Do you think she's having a terrible time?"

"Confessing?" He laughed. "From what I have learned of Stella I think she will make of it a good time. She will not weep because weeping places her kind of woman at a disadvantage. With a break in her voice she will say, 'Eduardo, my dear one, it has been a bitterness which I knew not how to support. To my dear father I sent money sometimes, but it grieved me so much never to see my sister that I had to have her come here to be with us, even though she could not come as Laurie Fielding. So much I have wanted to be honest with you, my darling.' " The absurd mimicry ended. "And Eduardo, the admirable fool, will feel her pain much more than she is capable of feeling it herself."

"You're cruel, Felipe!"

"Do you know," he said, as if in surprise, "that you have made me cruel? Three months ago it would not have occurred to me to carve up that pseudo-Tintoretto. I would merely have told Maybury it was a fake and advised him to look for a new employer. But the friendship you had for him. . . ."

"Haven't you realized," she interrupted, sitting up straight, "why I had to ask you to re-examine the picture? Cedric didn't know Stella, but he'd heard about her from my father and me. He knew me as Laurie Fielding."

Felipe almost glared. "Was he a cad as well as a fool—that man? Did he threaten you?"

"No, but he was going to wait on here, and see Stella. I was frantic, but if I'd had an inkling that the thing was a fraud I'd have told him so."

"Ah, so that was it. And that was the reason you would not give me your promise to see no more of him. Laurie," he demanded earnestly, "you have not loved this man—even a little?"

"Not even a little."

"I believe you now—I could not, then. It is strange how one small fact—that you are Stella's sister—makes all the pieces fall into place. I should have gone to England earlier, but I would not leave till I had seen Maybury off the island."

Laurie dug back into her cushion. From where she lay she could see the shivering tips of the great palm branches which hung over the shelter, a slope of grass, a tangle of rust-red bougainvillaea and the distant, shimmering sea which was a deeper, more solid blue than the sky. And against the green and the blue she could see Felipe's mahogany-tanned profile, arrogant, slightly hawk-nosed and beloved. He was here, within her hand's reach. She had the right to caress the lean jaw, to offer her lips. The joy and glory of it!

She paused in her delight to question what it was that lay like a grain of grit in her consciousness. And it came to her forcibly, like a muffled blow. Odd that she had not thought of it before, but the knowledge of being loved by Felipe had driven all else away—for a while, at any rate.

His quietness was suddenly irksome. What was he meditating so sternly? He had said he loved her and from Felipe, that was enough; much more than she had ever dared hope for.

He leaned closer, said peremptorily, "Why are you staring at me like that?"

"Was I staring?" With studied casualness, she queried, "Felipe, what did you do with Senhora Queira?"

"Corina?" He sounded startled. "I left her in England with my cousins. Why do you ask?"

"There was gossip about you. It was rumoured that you and she were going to be married."

"So?" He elevated his brow, "You were insanely jealous, I hope."

"I was," she admitted. "Didn't you . . . weren't you. . . ."

"I was not!" He gave her a small, sharp smile. "There has never been anyone but you,*querida*. I have enjoyed the company of Corina because she is interested in things which bore most of these women. Her husband was the friend of us all, and we pitied her when she lost him after so brief a marriage. For a Portuguese woman she has advanced ideas, but I doubt whether she has the mental stamina necessary to put them to action. I would have liked her to marry again—someone else, of course!—but she was reserved about that."

Reserved because he had made it too plain that he was not in the market, guessed Laurie in quick elation. Darling Felipe.

"She invited me to a picnic while you were away." she said.

"I suggest that she be friendly with you. Corina is not blind. From remarks she made when we were in London I would say she understood how I was feeling about you. She mentioned that she wished she had taken the trouble to become intimate with you, but she is unusually cold of nature. It is my opinion that she will be happy in England."

"Is she staying there?"

He smiled exuberantly. "I have much to tell you about that. Corina fancies herself as founder and organizer, in Portugal, of a Home such as the one in which you trained. She will learn much about the subject in England. I was pondering, when you gazed at me so earnestly just now, whether we could utilize that house which was my mother's for such a Home; I could not persuade my heart to sell it. It could be converted and those grounds are really superb for children. That is something with which, I am sure, my mother would have agreed, and in which you would find real enjoyment, eh, *Laurita mia?*

She glowed quietly. "The Marian Barreiro Home. I know people who would get it going. You're the sweetest man in the world, Felipe!"

"Cruel and sweet." He nodded, blandly accepting the combination. "That good father of yours gave me messages. You wish to hear them?"

"Later—so long as I know that he's well. He deserves more attention than I can give him just now. What about your lunch, Felipe?"

"Already the anxious wife! Presently we will go to the Palacio for tea, but first I must write a note for Eduardo. As your only male relative in the island he will have duties to perform."

"But not yet!"

"This very day. Tonight we must announce our engagement, and I will leave it to him to issue invitations. We will marry here in Mondego and fly afterwards to Europe."

" You go too fast. We're different now. We have to get acquainted all over again."

He took both her hands in his and kissed them. "We are no different. It was with you that I fell in love, not Stella's sister. I had plans from the start. When Stella and Eduardo were going away I thought at once that I must have you at Villa Barreiro." A humurous shrug. "So I send the bailiff on leave, because his is one of the best houses. That young man was amazed and gratified that I thought so well of him to give him two vacations in one year! Can you guess what I imagined then?"

Her eyes shone with love. "No, darling. Tell me."

"I saw us very happy I would teach you some Portuguese and we whould have much fun over it. I would also perhaps teach you some elementary love. We would explore each other till such simple love was no longer enough, and the time would come when I would take you in my arms, like so. . . ." He laughed with a gentle passion as he drew her up with him. "You would cling to me—how you comprehend, my pigeon!—and I would murmur, *'Meu amor, como tu es bela.'* And then I would kiss you."

After that kiss they stood very close, looking down over the greenness, the rust-red of the bougainvillaea, and the sea.

"It is a very lovely world," he said, "which can hold all this, and you, too. Say you love me, Laurie. Say it."

"I love you more than life," she said simply.

"You are not afraid of me?"

"Can there be fear, where there's love?"

He smiled with tender mockery. "Ah, she is also a philosopher. What else shall I learn about the mysterious heart of this white oleander, I wonder? I cannot wait!

Laurie did not answer. She was looking into the future, all heaven in her eyes.